CLAIMED BY MAGIC

BOOK TWO OF THE BAINE CHRONICLES: FENRIS'S STORY

JASMINE WALT

DYNAMO PRESS

Cover illustration by Judah Dobin

Cover typography by Rebecca Frank

Edited by Mary Burnett

Electronic edition, 2017. If you want to be notified when Jasmine's next novel is released and get access to exclusive contests, giveaways, and freebies, sign up for her mailing list here. Your email address will never be shared and you can unsubscribe at any time.

1

MINA

"Come on," Fenris gently coaxed. "You can do this."

Taking a deep breath, I lifted my face to the pale blue sky and focused my senses. In my small backyard, the plants were only surviving due to diligent watering—but the rosebush climbing up from the other side of the fence was starting to brown, its blossoms shriveling up. My tiny herb garden was burning up in the heat. The unusual dry spell worried the farmers, especially after the previous bad year.

I can make this better.

My magic hummed just under the surface of my skin. I quietly chanted the Words Fenris had taught me, careful to keep my voice down so the neighbors wouldn't hear. My fence was high enough that nobody could look in from inside their house, but I was in no hurry to upset the residents of Abbsville by revealing I wasn't a human like the rest of them.

Slowly, clouds began gathering in the nearly clear sky. Excitement buzzed in my veins, and I had to clamp down on it, to force myself to focus lest I put too much magic into the weather spell. I wanted the squall to look as natural as possible.

If I overdid it, the rain would come down in a sudden torrent and cause more harm than good.

A gentle rainfall, I told the magic as I continued chanting the spell. *Slow, gentle, and nourishing.*

"That's it," Fenris murmured as the air around us began to cool. "You're almost there."

The breeze began to stir around us, whispering against my skin as it played with the blonde hair hanging loose around my shoulders. The sky grew darker as clouds crept over it, blocking out the bright sun. A drop of rain landed on my nose.

"Excellent," Fenris said as the rain began to come down in earnest. "You've got this, Mina. Next time, you will be able to do this spell by yourself."

I beamed at him as the soft rainfall started to moisten the dry ground—and my hair and clothes, I realized, as I'd not brought out an umbrella. But instead of running inside, I turned my face upward again and spread my arms wide, embracing the small storm. Triumph glowed in my chest as the rain fell on my skin, cool and refreshing and so very welcome after these weeks of drought.

"This is amazing." I laughed, spinning in a circle. I was giddy, like a child witnessing her first rainfall, and I found myself caught up in an unexpected bout of whimsy.

"*You* are amazing." Chuckling, Fenris snagged me about the waist and brought me close. His yellow eyes were glowing, as they always did, with preternatural light, but they softened as they roamed over my face. "So beautiful," he murmured, leaning in. His lips brushed mine, and my body lit up, the rain instantly forgotten. Closing my eyes, I wrapped my arms around his strong neck and kissed him back, reveling in the sensation. I didn't have to hide anything from him, didn't have to worry about what he might think—

Fenris lifted his head, nostrils flaring. "Someone is about to arrive. With an injured animal."

I held in a sigh, sliding from his embrace. Sure enough, Mr. Provence, one of the local farmers, came rushing around the corner —patients and customers always used the back entrance, which led straight into my tiny surgery. His short brown hair was sticking up every which way despite the rain, as if he'd been running his hands through it agitatedly, and his eyes were wide with worry.

"Miss Hollin," he said, relief evident in his voice. "Thank the Ur-God you're here. My prize billy goat is badly injured. I'm worried he won't make it, and I was counting on the breeding fees."

My warm, fuzzy feelings evaporated instantly. "Did you bring the animal with you?"

"He's in the bed of my steamtruck, out front. I...I was afraid to move him again."

Fenris and I exchanged a look, and I hurried inside to grab a small stretcher before meeting the farmer out by his steamtruck. The animal was lying listlessly on his side, his white fur around the head and rib area matted with blood.

"What happened to him?" I demanded. I was expecting bite marks from some wild animal, but this...

"I accidentally hit him when I was backing up," Mr. Provence said guiltily. "He's small enough that I didn't see him in my rearview mirror. I know it's a slim chance, but I was hoping you could still save him. He's a long-haired breed, and you know how very rare and expensive those are. I can't afford to replace him if he doesn't make it."

"I will certainly see what I can do. Let's get him into the surgery."

Between the three of us, we managed to get the billy onto the stretcher, though he began bleating with pain the moment we tried to move him. *Poor creature,* I thought as we brought him inside. Probably had broken ribs, at the very least. And that bleeding around his head was anything but reassuring.

I informed the farmer that it was too early for a prognosis and that the goat would need to stay overnight. Once he was safely gone, promising to return late the next morning, I got to work in the surgery with Fenris. Chanting the diagnostic spell he'd taught me, I gently, carefully, patted down the billy goat. As I did so, a glowing haze formed over the animal's body, delineating bones and ligaments, blood vessels and organs. I was seeing inside his body, and...

"Three broken ribs," I murmured. "Bleeding from the liver. And the brain." My heart sank.

"We'll handle this together," Fenris said, twining his fingers with my own. "The brain is the most urgent and requires finesse. I'll take the lead there, while you concentrate on the ribs and liver. I'll call on you in case I need to draw strength."

Nodding, I let Fenris turn his attention to the brain while I focused on what I knew I could handle most easily—the ribs. One of them was stabbing into the liver. Magic flowed down my fingertips and into the abused bones, gradually knitting them back together. I gritted my teeth as sympathetic pain flared down my own abdomen—the cost of performing healing magic. Very few trained mages wasted their efforts on animals when there were never enough qualified healers to tend mages and humans. But from my earliest memories, I had always been drawn to animals and felt they deserved healing magic as much as their owners.

Finally, the liver bleed was healed and the blood clots reabsorbed. The goat's ribs were knitted together, and Fenris had successfully healed the brain injury. All the pain finally faded away, and I sighed in relief. I was exhausted, and even Fenris looked a bit tired.

"There," he said, stroking the billy goat's head. "All better now, right?"

The billy opened his eyes, then bleated in alarm as he beheld Fenris. "Ow!" Fenris cried as the goat bit him on the arm. "Ungrateful creature!"

I laughed, coming forward to soothe the poor animal as Fenris backed away. "He's probably just frightened of your wolfish nature," I said, stroking the goat and sending calming magic into him. The billy settled beneath my hands, though he continued to glare balefully at Fenris. "And he's just been through an ordeal, besides."

"I suppose," Fenris said, still sounding a bit miffed. "I'll go make some tea while you finish up with him."

Shaking my head, I cleaned the blood from the billy's fur, then settled him into my largest cage with blankets and water, where he would remain until the next morning. He might be healed, but he still needed to rest after all that trauma. I'd have to remember to apply some bandages before his owner came back so the magical healing would not be quite so obvious. But that could wait, since the billy might gnaw them off overnight.

Satisfied that my patient was comfortable, I cleaned up the surgery, then went out to the living room where Fenris sat, drinking from one of the cups already.

The tomcat I'd rescued was sitting on the kitchen table across the room, glaring suspiciously—he hadn't warmed up to Fenris yet and was unlikely to come near me while the wolf shifter was here. Fenris had also made sandwiches, I saw, noting the two plates on the coffee table—one was empty, with nothing but crumbs, and the other had a single sandwich on it.

"You're going to have to get over it sometime," I said, rubbing the cat behind the ears. He swatted at me, and I tsked. "You can't be mad just because I like to have company over."

The cat ignored me and began licking himself. Knowing I

was dismissed, I turned to Fenris instead. "Am I out of cold cuts and bread, then?" I teased as I sat down next to him. Shifters had very large appetites—Fenris would need far more than one sandwich to sate him after all that healing.

He gave me a sheepish smile. "I'm afraid so. I'll buy you more from the general store."

"No need," I said, taking his free hand in mine. "Your help today was thanks enough." I turned his hand over, my fingers playing across the roughened skin as I searched for the bite. But there was no trace of it. "Healed already," I murmured. "Amazing."

"Mostly," Fenris said, smiling. "One of the perks of being a shifter. But a kiss would still help make it feel better."

I kissed his hand, right where the bite had been. Fenris's eyes darkened, and he set down his teacup. "Not there," he growled, tangling his fingers with mine. He pulled me close until I was practically sitting in his lap. "Here."

His lips found mine, and I kissed him deeply, my exhaustion forgotten. The woodsy scent of him filled my head as warmth spread through my limbs, stoking the fires of sexual hunger that had awoken in the back of my mind the moment I'd met him. I slid my hands over his broad shoulders and down his chest, enjoying the feel of the powerful muscles beneath his tunic. From experience, I knew just how built he was beneath his clothes, how effortless it was for him to scoop me up in his arms as if I weighed nothing...

"Take me to bed," I murmured against his mouth. "I don't have any patients left for the day. You can stay the night."

Fenris chuckled. "Eager, are we?" His hand skimmed beneath my blouse, and my breath caught as his thumb brushed the underside of my breast. "There will be gossip, you know." He trailed kisses along the edge of my jaw, making a path toward my ear.

"There already is." I gasped as he bit down on my earlobe. "Everybody is wondering when you are going to propose to me."

Fenris laughed, scooping me up in his arms. "I have to tend to my horses, so I can't stay the night. But," he added, his voice dipping low with sensual promise, "there is no reason why I can't tend to you first."

2

MINA

Fenris carried me to the bedroom, where he stripped me naked and proceeded to ravish me like a man starved. His hot mouth and skilled hands drove me to the edge repeatedly, finding my sweet spots with a deftness that spoke of experience.

"Let me touch you," I panted after the fourth climax.

Fenris lifted his head from between my legs, his yellow eyes blazing with lust. Rising onto his knees, he undid his tunic belt, then pulled the tunic over his head, leaving him bare from the waist up. My mouth practically watered at the sight of him there, half naked, and I knelt on the bed before him so I could run my hands over his bare chest. His muscles flexed beneath my hands as they traveled down his abdomen, the hot skin and crisp hairs teasing my palms. And when my fingertips finally reached the waistband of his pants, my breath hitched in my throat.

"Mina—"

I slid my right hand beneath the waistband and cupped his balls. Fenris made a low groan deep in his throat as I squeezed gently. "It's my turn," I breathed into his ear as I massaged him. I licked his earlobe, and his right arm banded around my waist, as if he wanted to keep me exactly where I was.

"Higher," he growled, the sound reverberating through his chest, which was pressed up against mine. I obliged, letting my hand drift upward. He groaned again as I wrapped my fingers around his impressive length and began to stroke him. Using my free hand, I slid his pants down until they pooled around his knees. He kicked them off the rest of the way, then allowed me to push him back onto the bed.

I spent the rest of the evening exploring his body, finding out how he liked to be stroked, where he liked to be touched. It turned out that his neck was quite sensitive, and that licking him in certain spots produced the most interesting sounds. And when he finally came, my name a roar on his lips, it filled me with such a heady sense of power that for a moment I was quite speechless.

"You're magnificent," he said afterward, stroking my hair as we cuddled. "I have no idea how I resisted you for so long."

I chuckled, nuzzling his neck. "It seems like wasted time, doesn't it?"

We snuggled for a few more minutes, then dressed and went back out to the kitchen for a snack. I hadn't eaten dinner, and the sandwich Fenris had made me was still waiting on the coffee table, forgotten. I heated some leftovers from last night's dinner, and as we ate, we went over our plans to reclaim my true name and recover the fortune I had relinquished when I fled my hometown nearly thirteen years ago. Haralis, the city of my childhood, was in Innarta, a southern state all the way on the other side of the Federation. From Abbsville, in the northwest, it would be a long journey to the Eastern Seaboard.

I had no idea if returning to Haralis would be dangerous, since I didn't know if my cousin had survived the fall after I pushed him down the stairs that fateful night. I might have to stand trial, and since there had been no other witnesses, who knew how that would end?

Even so, anything was better than this uncertainty. I had to confront my past if I wanted to enjoy my future without having to skulk and hide.

"Barrla has agreed to take care of the cat and my horse during our journey," I said. She liked animals nearly as much as I did, and as my best friend, she was the person I relied on for such things. "Have you found someone to look after your horses yet?"

Fenris nodded. "They'll be staying with the breeder I bought them from," he said. "I've also asked Marris to come by to check on the garden. I've put out spells to keep rabbits and other pests away, but it never hurts to have someone check."

I chewed on my lip. "I am worried about leaving Abbsville for so long," I confessed. "These farmers really depend on me. Or rather, their animals do. What if there is another infection, like we had last month?"

"You were never going to settle here permanently," Fenris reminded me. "The people of Abbsville managed to get on without a resident veterinarian before your arrival, and they will no doubt survive for the few weeks we will be gone."

I nodded. "There is a vet in the next town over if they need one," I said. "He's not bad—for a human without magic, that is. Have you already figured out the best route to get to Innarta, then?"

"I've been making inquiries," he said, "and the fastest way is by airship. We can fly from Willowdale to Deros, and catch a connecting flight that will take us straight to Innarta."

"I've never flown on an airship before," I said. "When I ran away from home, I took steambuses." Those trips had been very long and arduous, and though I was a little apprehensive about flying, I was also relieved we wouldn't be crammed on a bus for such a long distance. I still had vivid memories of snoring and overweight passengers crowding me, the smell of cheap sausage and garlic in suffocating heat, and grimy public lavatories. None of which would suit Fenris, I suspected.

"You will love flying," Fenris assured me. "The views are spectacular, once you get into the air. And it is not all that dangerous, though I will teach you the levitating spell before we depart, just in case. A good friend of mine was in a crash not long ago, and that spell saved him."

I shuddered at the thought of crashing. "Yes, please. I would like to learn levitation, in any case, it could have lots of useful applications." Like getting frightened kittens down from tree limbs, or hiding things on top of a high bookcase. Though I would have to be discreet if I used such a spell in public...

"Then you shall learn. And I will buy the tickets tomorrow," Fenris promised.

We chatted over our food a bit longer before I reluctantly walked Fenris to the door. He kissed me once more, then saddled up his gelding and rode off into the night. As I leaned against the windowsill, watching him ride off, I couldn't help thinking that if we were married, we would be able to spend the nights together much more easily.

We've only known each other a few weeks, I chided myself. *Marriage is forever, and the last thing you should be thinking about right now.*

No, it was better to take it slow. This was the first real relationship I'd ever had, and though I was very fond of Fenris, there were still many things I did not know about him. Secrets I would need to uncover, if we were to take things any further.

But for now, Fenris's secrets could stay buried. Reclaiming my identity and inheritance was the top priority, and I could not let anything distract me from that goal.

3

FENRIS

The next morning arrived, and with it came another letter from Mina's family lawyer, forwarded by the same tobacconist in the state capital. The heavy, cream-colored envelope looked strangely ominous, and even though it had only been hours since I'd last seen Mina, I found myself saddling up my stallion to go see her again. The letter was really for her, after all, even if I was making the inquiries under a false name, pretending to be a buyer for her late grandmother's mansion. It would be rude to read it without her.

A brisk canter shortened the ride to less than ten minutes. In no time at all, I swung down from the saddle in front of her modest home. As I led my horse into her small backyard stable, I caught the sound of conversation. Two young females and Mina. My shoulders tensed at the strain in her voice, and I hurriedly entered through the unlocked front door.

"Your face in this guise is certainly very different from your real one," one of the visitors was saying, and it did not sound like a compliment. "But then, older mages do prefer to look youthful, don't they?"

I knew that voice. Clostina, the Watawis Chief Mage's granddaughter, whom we had first met when Mina went to register as a mage in the state. Next to Clostina sat another mage, also young and pretty. Both looked startled, and not altogether pleased, at my unexpected intrusion.

"Fenris!" Mina jumped up from where she was sitting on the couch, her face the picture of surprise. But beneath the mask, I could scent her relief and anxiety—she had been caught just as unawares by this visit as I had.

"Do you usually let shifters barge into your house unannounced?" Clostina's friend said, somehow managing to look down her straight nose at me while remaining seated.

"Mr. Shelton is a valued client and a good friend," Mina said briskly. Even though she did not turn on the old-lady mage illusion, she changed her demeanor to that of a haughty elder. "And it is my own business who I do and do not allow into my house."

"I suppose so," Clostina said dubiously, "though perhaps you should ask your client to come back later, when we are finished?"

The meaningful tone suggested that what she wanted to say was for mage ears only, but Mina merely shrugged. "You said you would only be a few minutes, and it would be rude of me to send Mr. Shelton away when he does, in fact, have an appointment. Your horse is out back waiting for me, is he not?" She lifted an eyebrow.

I nodded, hiding a smile at Mina's quick thinking. "He is, with a lame foot."

Clostina let out an exasperated sigh. "Very well then, but don't blame us if the whole town learns you are a mage or someone tries to rob you. The reason for my visit," she announced, reaching into her wide sleeve, "is to bring your yearly allotment of gold." She withdrew a sizable leather pouch and handed it to Mina. Mina's face was inscrutable, but the change in her scent told me she was nonplussed by this turn of events. "From the, uh, *simple* way you live here, I can tell you have not resorted to producing any gold of your own."

"Of course I haven't," Mina replied tartly. "I am perfectly aware it would be highly illegal, and we would have rampant inflation if every mage produced their own coin. But however poor I may look at present, I am hardly in need of such an offering." She made no move to take the pouch.

"Nonsense." Clostina smiled, showing her perfect white teeth. "I created these particular coins myself, you know. This year, the allotment is fifty gold coins for every full-fledged mage in the state and twenty-four for apprentices. There is enough here for both you and the handsome apprentice you brought to the ball. Surely he will want his share, even if you do not."

"Well, it's hardly worth arguing over," Mina said, sounding bored as she finally took the pouch. She tied it to her belt, then took the receipt and pen Clostina handed to her and signed.

"And where is that apprentice of yours, anyway?" the other mage asked, looking around curiously. "I wasn't at the ball, and was hoping for the chance to meet him." I had to suppress a smile—he was right there, in the room, but they ignored me completely.

"He is visiting with family," Mina said, "and will be gone for some weeks, I'm afraid. Since this is such a small space, he does not stay around all the time."

"How is that billy goat that came in yesterday?" I asked to distract the mages before they could ask more questions about my fictitious alter ego. "He seemed in very bad shape."

"Much better, but I should check on him," Mina said, rising from the couch. "His owner will be coming by to pick him up soon. Will you excuse me, ladies?"

Without awaiting a reply, she went through the connecting door into the surgery. The two mages exchanged a glance, then followed her inside.

"There you are," Mina said as the billy goat bleated. She crouched in front of the cage and unlocked it to pour some feed into the goat's bowl. "You are doing much better, aren't you?" she crooned, patting the goat's head.

"By the Lady," Clostina said, her eyes wide as she looked around and sniffed the goat's distinctive aroma. "You have really been taking this bet quite seriously, haven't you? Wasting your magic on animals that don't even belong to you?"

Mina closed the cage and rose to her full height. "The bet, as it turns out, is not off," she said in a cold voice. "My friend and I have agreed to continue it, since the humans are still in the dark about my identity. Only my shifter friend here knows the truth, and he has already agreed to keep his silence." She stroked a hand down my arm, smiling. "Haven't you, Mr. Shelton?"

"I certainly have," I said, smiling back. "I, for one, greatly appreciate you using your abilities to care for the animals, and would hate to see you leave. My lips are sealed."

Clostina did not look entirely convinced, but she couldn't very well refute Mina—she'd already proven herself to be a mage, and from the way Clostina was looking around, she could see the signs of magic in use everywhere. The two mages pestered Mina for a bit longer, but eventually, disappointed, they took their leave.

"Thank you," Mina said fervently when they were finally gone. "I'm so glad you came by."

"Me too," I said, wrapping my arms around her as she hugged me. Not that I had done anything, really, but my presence had been enough of a distraction that Clostina had not looked too closely. She might be young, but she was not stupid, not by a long shot. If she put her mind to it, she might notice that the selfless animal doctor and the flirtatious old-lady mage didn't make for a consistent character, even amongst the most eccentric mages. Since Mina wasn't ready to reveal the truth to Abbsville, it was best Clostina not find out either.

I was just dipping my head to kiss her when someone else knocked on the door. "Barrla," I murmured, frowning at the door. I could scent her clearly—a pleasant combination of rose and spices, the latter no doubt from her father's store. Accompanying that scent was something sugary and delicious. "With freshly baked cookies, I believe."

"Well, I can't very well turn *those* away, now can I?"

Smiling, Mina extricated herself from my arms and went to answer the door. Barrla was standing outside, her golden-red hair swept back from her pretty face into a ponytail. She wore a blue-and-white checkered dress, and that divine smell wafted from a basket slung over her arm. I hadn't eaten much today, and my mouth watered as the two of them hugged and exchanged greetings.

"Well, well." Barrla's blue eyes lit up as she noticed me standing just inside. "And I thought *I* was calling on you a bit early. Or have you decided to move in with Mina, Mr. Shelton?" She winked at me.

Mina's cheeks colored. "We're not quite *that* close yet."

"Mmm." Barrla set her basket down on the counter and lifted the cloth. For a moment, I thought she would grill us more about our relationship, but she changed the subject to something far worse. "I saw a couple of mages come by earlier. What did they want with you?"

Mina's scent changed, growing sharp with anxiety. But she calmly took a cookie from the basket, as though nothing was wrong, and I followed suit. Chocolate chip and soft enough that it melted on my tongue when I took the first bite.

"I met them in town the other week," Mina said in a casual tone, "and they decided to visit me as they were passing through Abbsville. One of them is curious about my veterinary practice and asked me to show her around the surgery." She took a bite of her cookie, then closed her eyes. "Oh, these are very good."

"Yes," I agreed, noticing Barrla didn't seem convinced by Mina's explanation. "You're a great baker, Barrla. Have you considered bringing a sample of these over to Marris's house? I'm sure he would appreciate them."

Barrla shrugged. "Marris wouldn't want me coming around his farm to bother him over a few treats," she said. "He had a crush on me when we were still in the schoolroom, but he's past that now. With his father gone, he has his hands full."

"That may be so, but I don't think Marris is so busy that he would turn away a pretty girl on his doorstep," Mina said encouragingly. "You know what they say—the way to a man's heart is through his stomach."

Barrla raised an eyebrow. "And when did I say I was interested in Marris's heart?"

"It's just as well that you are not," I said, reaching for another cookie. "Marris is a good fellow, but perhaps not the best choice for a boyfriend or husband. He has too much of a thirst for adventure."

"I like adventure," Barrla said, playing right into my hands. I had to hide a smile. "Perhaps I'll go off in search of some today." She covered the basket, then hooked it over her arm. "I can see you two were in the middle of something, so I'll be on my way. Don't forget to come to the next book club meeting, Mina," she added. "We've been missing you."

"I'll do my best," Mina promised, "but likely there won't be time before I have to leave."

She thanked Barrla for agreeing to take the cat, promising to bring him by when it was time, and Barrla left with a thoughtful expression on her face. Mina shook her head at me as she closed the door. "I didn't realize you were fond of playing matchmaker," she said, sounding amused.

I gave her a crooked smile. "Perhaps if she and Marris get together, she will stop pining for a shifter lover."

Mina laughed. "So you know about that, do you?"

"I saw one of those novels sitting on the store counter, and her interest in me was obvious." I slid my arms around Mina. "Since I only have eyes for you, it would be in my best interests to point Barrla in a different direction."

"A wise plan. Now, what is the real reason for your visit? Is your horse really injured, or did you just miss me?"

I chuckled at her teasing smile. "I did miss you, but my horse is in fine health. I came because I received another letter from your family lawyer."

The smile vanished instantly. "What does it say?"

I pulled the letter from my tunic pocket and handed it to her. "Let's read it together."

4

MINA

Fenris and I sat down at the kitchen table so I could open the letter. I slit the envelope with a scalpel, then unfolded the heavy paper with a much calmer hand than I would have a few weeks ago. Now that I'd decided to confront my past, the old anxiety and fear had loosened their claws on my mind to some extent. Yes, I was dreading the inevitable reunion with my relatives, but that didn't mean I had to let that dread control me.

If I did, if I kept running like I'd done all these years, then they would win. And I couldn't allow that to happen.

"It's a follow-up to the last letter he sent," I said as I scanned it. A few weeks ago, Fenris had penned a letter to Domich Ransome, my family lawyer, under an assumed name, asking whether my grandmother's mansion was for sale. The lawyer had responded promptly, letting us know the mansion might be on the market very soon, that they were waiting for the thirteen-year statute to expire on Tamina Marton, the last owner's missing heiress.

That missing heiress was far from dead, however. She was sitting right here, clutching this second letter, plotting how to wrest back an inheritance she should never have had to fight for in the first place.

Reining in my anger, I turned my attention back to the letter. "I urge you to make an offer as soon as possible," I read aloud to Fenris. "This historic beachfront property will not remain on the market for long. The statutory thirteen years the family has been waiting to declare Miss Tamina Marton dead is expiring in just three weeks—"

Cold horror filled me, and I dropped the letter as if it had scalded me. "Three weeks?" I exclaimed to Fenris, whose expression had turned quite serious. "That's not a very long time at all!"

"No, it is not," he said gravely. "We should depart as soon as possible to beat that deadline. But first, let's read the rest of the letter."

I nodded, taking a deep breath to calm myself. In the next paragraph, Mr. Ransome reiterated his expectation that the Marton mansion would come on the market only days after my legal "death" and would be snatched up very quickly by one of several prospective buyers who, he implied, were already lining up. He assured Fenris that should he be interested in making an offer now, he would be happy to act as a go-between for him and the Cantorin family—the aunt and uncle who had taken me in. Of course, he added, Mr. Vanley Cantorin, the family's only son, might yet wish to claim the mansion for himself, so the sale was not entirely certain. But a large enough offer from Fenris might be incentive enough to sway the young heir.

"That bastard," I fumed, setting down the letter. Finally, I knew Vanley was alive—that I had not managed to kill him my last evening in Haralis. But my relief was overshadowed by anger. "Over my dead body will I let Vanley squat in my grandmother's mansion!"

"We shall not let it come to that," Fenris assured me. "It is a good thing we have learned about this in time—thirteen years is actually on the long side. Many states only wait seven years to presume someone dead."

I shook my head. "I shouldn't be so surprised. Aunt Allira and Uncle Bobb have never thought very highly of me, and they have no reason to think I'm coming back. For all I know, they really do think I'm dead after all these years."

"Are you sure you're ready for this confrontation?" Fenris asked. "If this is only about getting vengeance against Vanley for what he did to you, there are other ways." His tone turned ominous, and I had a feeling he'd spent considerable time thinking up ways to punish my cousin for the way he'd abused me.

"It's not just about vengeance, or even the fortune," I tried to explain. Though both would be very sweet when I finally got them, I admitted silently. "There are many treasured Marton heirlooms in my grandmother's house that my relatives don't care one whit about. After all, it's not *their* ancestors—the only reason they're benefiting is because Aunt Allira is my mother's sister, and they were never close to begin with. If they inherit the estate, it will just be money to them. They will gladly sell everything to the highest bidder. And they should not be allowed to profit off me after treating me so horribly," I declared, setting my jaw. "If not vengeance, I should at least get justice."

"I agree completely." Fenris reached across the table to squeeze my hand. "I'll arrange for us to be on the next flight to Innarta, and I'll book us a good hotel, too."

"Get us rooms at the Black Horse, if you can. It's the best hotel in Haralis." Haralis was the capital of Innarta, where I had spent many happy childhood years before being driven away from my home. "I'll also need better clothes," I said ruefully, looking down at myself. If I was going to return home as a wealthy mage heiress reclaiming her patrimony, I could not dress like a pauper. The Mages Guild wouldn't take me seriously if I came to them as Mina Hollin, small-town veterinarian. I had to leave my comfortable jeans behind and dress up as Tamina Marton, the last scion of a distinguished and wealthy line of mages.

"I agree," Fenris said. "You won't be able to wear robes since you are not a trained mage or apprentice, but there is no reason why we can't purchase some fashionable attire in Willowdale before catching our flight."

I shrugged. "I never cared much for apprentice robes anyway." They were always so dull, made from that dun-colored fabric, and unflattering on almost everyone. Wearing them for ten whole years, the average length of an apprenticeship, was not at all enticing.

"You are not the first woman to say so," Fenris said with a smile, his eyes twinkling as though he were laughing at some inside joke. "Let's get some pen and paper and make a list. There is much to be done before we depart."

5

MINA

After Fenris left to book the tickets for the first available flight, I tried to busy myself about the house, tidying things up and caring for my mare and the goat that was still recovering in my surgery. But after slapping some bandages on him, there was very little to do—I wasn't going to bring any of my things on the trip, the house was fairly clean already, and there were no patients on the schedule this morning.

The goat's owner broke up the monotony when he came to pick up the animal and thanked me profusely for his amazing recovery. He left three dozen eggs on my counter as payment. As I stared at the offering, I lamented that it wasn't coin. I would be able to take coin on the trip, but these eggs might spoil if I was gone for too long. I would have to give them away, perhaps to Barrla. She, at least, could use them to bake more cookies.

Then I remembered it didn't matter—for the first time in years, I had plenty of gold. My gaze went to the pouch Clostina had left for me, still sitting on the coffee table. I scooped it up, weighing the heavy purse in my hand. I could not leave a small fortune around the house while I was gone, even if break-ins were almost unheard of around Abbsville. A single gold coin would settle my account at the general store and prepay for the next quarter. I would also take some on my trip, but the rest needed to be hidden somewhere.

After roughly estimating my travel costs and doubling the sum to be on the safe side, I removed half the coins and put them in my old leather purse, which I packed in my duffel bag for the trip. The rest I left in Clostina's pouch, which I hid in a sack of specialty dog food, one of several I kept in my surgery for dogs with dietary issues. I cut a slit in the back to insert the pouch, then carefully mended it using a spell Fenris had taught me to sew wounds. It worked just as seamlessly on burlap as it did on flesh, closing the bag so smoothly I couldn't tell it had been sliced open in the first place.

Satisfied with my precautions, I put on my slicker and rain boots, then dropped the last gold coin in my pocket and walked over to the general store. The rain lightly pattered against my hood, and I smiled, pleased it was still coming down. *I* had done this with *my* magic, and I couldn't help feeling incredibly proud of that fact.

"Hey, Mina," Barrla said with a smile when I stepped into the store. She was ringing up a customer—there were quite a few around, probably all driven indoors by the rain. "Finished up with your morning patient?"

The saucy wink she gave me left no doubt in my mind as to which "morning patient" she was referring to. Holding back a grin, I leaned my hip against the counter. "Just about. Did you ever get around to making that 'morning delivery?'"

Barrla's cheeks turned the faintest shade of pink. "I was delayed by the rain," she said, turning her blue eyes to the window.

"It's quite fortuitous, this storm," Mr. Tilin, Abbsville's resident carpenter, commented. "I wasn't certain my cabbages would survive."

"Oh yes, it's a lifesaver," a woman perusing the baking goods agreed. "I prayed to the Ur-God for rain—I think it helped."

Barrla finished with the customer. While the others continued talking about the weather, I approached her. "I'd like to put this on my account," I said, handing her my coin.

Barrla's eyebrows rose. "That's a pretty piece of metal," she said, holding it up and admiring its glint. I gave her a warning look, but before she could ask about it, the door opened, bringing in the wind and the rain. Barrla's eyes narrowed with dislike, and I turned to see Roor standing in the entrance, a scowl on his face. My stomach dropped—my former suitor had a bandage wrapped around his head, and he looked extremely unhappy to see me. I held my breath, bracing for a confrontation.

But he simply walked right by, refusing to look at me.

I let out a quiet sigh of relief as he lumbered past, no doubt moving carefully because of his healing ribs. But the moment was short-lived.

"Mr. Roor, if you're going to come into my store, I expect you to show some manners," Barrla said sharply. "How dare you walk right past this counter and act as if we don't exist!"

Roor turned slowly, an ugly expression on his face. "This isn't your store," he sneered. "And I don't talk to witches." His mud-brown eyes raked over me briefly before he made to turn away again.

"*Witches?*" I echoed. "What in Recca are you talking about?" Goose bumps broke out across my skin—had he figured out the truth about me? Was he going to tell the rest of the town?

Roor snorted. "Playing coy, just like always, Mina. Weren't you just visited this morning by a couple of mages?"

"So *that's* where you got the gold coin," the woman in the baking section said. I gritted my teeth, fighting an uncharacteristic urge to strangle her.

"Accepting gold from mages?" Roor sneered. "Are you working as a spy for the Mages Guild, then?"

"Don't be ridiculous," Barrla snapped. "Mina would never stoop to that kind of work. And she's far too good for *you*, Ilain Roor." Roor's expression turned thunderous, but Barrla ignored his anger. "Besides, if Mina were a spy, the mages wouldn't visit her so openly, wearing robes and all. They would be more discreet."

"That's true," Mr. Tilin said, and the others murmured their agreement. Roor didn't look convinced, but he seemed to realize there was no point in pushing the argument further. With a scowl, he went about his business. I selected a jug of milk, some cheese, and bread, then hurriedly had Barrla ring up my purchases before Roor changed his mind and decided to harass me again.

As I walked home in the rain with my groceries, I felt dejected. I couldn't truly trust anyone in Abbsville aside from Fenris, and even he kept secrets from me. I wished I could confide my own secret to Barrla and my other local friends, but as things stood, the truth about my identity would always stand like an invisible barrier between us. Whenever Barrla defended me, as she had just done, I cringed with guilt inside.

Would Barrla even want to remain friends with me if she knew I was a mage? And was telling her the truth worth risking our friendship? I wasn't sure I wanted to find out.

6

FENRIS

"Thanks for coming out with us on such short notice," Marris called over his shoulder as we navigated the narrow forest path on horseback. "I know you're about to leave on a trip, but after all you've done for us, we wanted to show you this place before you left."

"It's not a problem." I'd already finished with most of my urgent errands for today—after my visit with Mina, I'd made a few calls on the local inn's telephone to arrange transport to Innarta and accommodation at the Black Horse in Haralis, then returned home to work on my burgeoning garden once the rainstorm let up.

But only a few minutes after the clouds had parted, Marris, Roth, and Cobil had shown up at my doorstep. Now I found myself riding through the woods with them, heading, I suspected, toward the secret mine I'd discovered some weeks back.

Yes, I thought as we passed through the glade where I'd spotted Marris and his friends as they'd snuck into town under the cover of darkness. I'd come back to this place in the light of day, then backtracked their scent to discover what they'd been up to.

We passed through a thicket of bushes onto a deer trail, which led to a side valley well hidden from the main path. This hidden vale was no doubt the reason why the mine had remained mostly untouched, especially since gold mining had been outlawed by the Federal government some two hundred years ago.

"My word," I said, injecting a note of surprise into my voice as we guided our horses into the valley toward some rocky cliffs. The cliffs were tucked into the grassy knolls that rolled into the base of the mountain range. "What is this place?"

"There's an old mine down here," Roth said, grinning. "It's where we've been getting the gold."

"Best-kept secret in the Abbsville area," Cobil said as we approached one of the cliffs, his voice filled with pride. "We discovered it by accident when we were just schoolboys, years ago. You're the first person we've shown this to."

We dismounted, and I let the men lead me to the padlocked door in the rock face. Marris fished a key from his pocket and unlocked the solid wooden door, then dragged it open. Beyond, a tunnel led further into the blackness of the cliff, and I nearly conjured a ball of flame to light the way before I remembered that Marris and his friends thought me a mere shifter.

Your magic lessons with Mina are making you sloppy. I had resolved to use magic as little as possible when I'd moved to Abbsville, but meeting Mina had changed things significantly. I could hardly abstain from using my powers while I was trying to teach her to use her own, and I had grown a little too comfortable reaching for my spells these past weeks. Now I waited with what patience I could muster while Cobil passed around torches, then lit them with matches from a tin in his pocket.

"This is quite a find," I told Marris as he showed me around the mine. They seemed proud of their discovery, along with the fact they had figured out how to mine the ore despite having no experience. I sniffed the air, stale but breathable, and lifted my torch to illuminate a sagging beam at the side of the tunnel.

"This place must be over two centuries old—look at these support beams." I touched one, and the wood gave slightly beneath my fingers. "Rotting. If this beam collapses, it could bring the entire ceiling down."

Cobil paled. "Is there any way to fix them? It would be a shame to leave all this gold down here." He gestured to the walls, where bits of ore gleamed all around us.

I shook my head. "Not easily, and certainly none of us have the experience to do so." I could do it with my magic, but I couldn't tell them that. Besides, I was trying to discourage them from further illegal activity. "Unless you are willing to risk bringing an outside mining specialist into your operation, which is highly inadvisable, I would not mine here again. What you have been doing to help your neighbors is admirable, but it is not worth your lives."

Marris and the others grumbled a bit, but in the end, they agreed safety was paramount. Having worked up an appetite, we left the mine and made a fire in a small clearing in the cliff's shadow. Cobil and Roth had brought down two pheasants on our way, so we roasted the birds for an impromptu lunch—or at least a snack that would hold me over until I returned home.

"So," Roth said as he polished off a pheasant leg, "looks like you and Mina are going steady now."

I swallowed the mouthful I was chewing. "We have been seeing each other, yes," I admitted. There was little point in denying it when the whole town kept abreast of everyone's comings and goings.

"You're one lucky bastard," Marris said, admiration glinting in his eyes. "I never thought Mina would let any man get close to her. Figures it would take a shifter to crack that nut." He winked.

"I am very lucky," I agreed, thinking about how good Mina had felt last night in my arms. I loved the way she'd looked at me —as if I were the only man in the world. And when she'd turned the tables and taken me into her hands...

"I hope you are not just taking advantage of her," Roth said, interrupting my train of thought. "Mina is a respectable woman."

I could have retorted that it was none of his business, but I could tell from his earnest expression that the question arose from genuine concern. "I would marry her in a heartbeat," I said, doing my best to push my heated thoughts away as my body began to react. I was only torturing myself by fantasizing about Mina when I wouldn't see her again until tomorrow at the earliest. "But it is up to the lady how far things go."

Cobil raised an eyebrow. "If I were in your shoes, I'd be carting her off to the nearest courthouse. That's the kind of woman you want to pin down tight before she gets away."

Part of me agreed with Cobil's sentiment wholeheartedly— but the larger part recognized that Mina might yet change her mind about me once she reentered society and instead choose to marry a more suitable partner. Sunaya and Iannis had a difficult enough relationship—Mina and I would face even more challenges, since she did not have the same clout as a Chief Mage, and unlike Sunaya, I was forced to pretend that I did not have magic.

"When I was last in Willowdale, I heard a jeweler who was creating counterfeit coins had been arrested," I said, deliberately changing the subject.

Marris's face darkened. "Yeah. He's already been sentenced —ironically, to work in the government's mines. I suppose it could have been worse, since counterfeiting is usually punished by hanging." There was a guilty look in his eyes. I was glad he knew, at least, just what risk they were all running. "He helped us convert the gold to coins. But I never used my name or told him where I lived, so we should still be safe."

I shook my head at his naivety. "I would not be so complacent," I warned. "The jeweler may have given the authorities a close description of you in exchange for leniency, and the fact that everyone in Abbsville was able to pay their taxes while so many neighboring towns were less fortunate may yet draw the attention of the investigating mages. It might be prudent if you made yourself scarce for a little while."

Marris stiffened. "I'm not going to run away with my tail between my legs like some coward. And besides, Barrla finally agreed to go on a date with me. I've been trying to get her attention for years."

I held in a sigh. It had been stupid of me to encourage Barrla's affections toward Marris when trouble loomed on the horizon. Perhaps my feelings for Mina had clouded my judgment.

"Barrla isn't going anywhere," Roth argued. "I'm sure she'd rather you stay safe, Marris, than go on a date with her and risk imprisonment."

"I agree," Cobil said. "I think we'd all do well to listen to Fenris. He's got more experience with mages and their ways than the three of us combined."

"You'd make the perfect leader for our little band," Roth said, a speculative look in his eyes. "We've been thinking about forming something like the Resistance, but different and better."

My eyebrows rose. "I have no intention of starting a rebellion—"

Marris waved my objection away, enthused again. "We're not trying to change the entire Federation," he argued. "We just want to protect our own. The Resistance was too big and easily corrupted, but this would just be something small and local. We'd remain independent, and we wouldn't be influenced by greed and selfish agendas."

"While I do consider the three of you friends, I think you're being a bit presumptuous," I said dryly. "There is much you don't know about me—I am not the kind of man to lead a revolution, even on a small scale." I'd already gotten myself into enough trouble with illegal activities. "While I have my own issues with the mage regime, not all of them are evil. This may be hard for you to believe, but there are mages in my own family tree, and I've even had a few as friends."

Marris's eyes about popped from his skull. "Are you serious? *Mages* as friends and relatives? I thought shifters hated mages!"

I nodded. "Many of us do...but as I said, there are a few mages in my lineage, and I do not share the hostile attitude of most shifters. It is true that mages as a class have been corrupted by their monopoly of power, and they tend to be oblivious to the interests of humans and shifters. But I am not willing to wage war on all mages simply for being who they are. They cannot help it any more than I can help being a shifter or you three being human."

"Well, if you really are that intimately acquainted with mages, it makes sense you've got a more nuanced view of them," Roth said reasonably. "I guess fighting against the mages is a losing proposition anyway."

"What if we call our group the League of Justice?" Marris asked suddenly, his face brightening. "Instead of fighting against mages, we can dedicate ourselves to righting wrongs, or preventing them from happening in the first place. Regardless of race."

"That sounds like a great idea to me," Cobil said. "Now that we have more than just humans living here." He winked at me. "Not that we have to stick to Abbsville—that would be boring.

We can operate in the entire state of Watawis, just like the Enforcers Guild does."

"Excellent idea." Marris turned his eager gaze to me. "Well? What do you say, Fenris?"

I pressed my lips together, hesitant to agree. I was about to leave for Innarta—embroiling myself in this new scheme was hardly a good idea. But I also couldn't leave these young men to blunder about by themselves—unless they had a guiding hand to steer them away from dangerous follies, their good intentions might soon come to grief. They had no idea what they were up against.

"I'll be leaving soon for at least a couple of weeks, out of state, to help Mina deal with a legal issue," I finally said, "but I will think about your suggestion in the meantime. Regardless of my answer," I added when they looked disappointed, "I want you all to promise me that whenever I am in town, you will bring news of injustices or problems to me for consultation *before* deciding on a plan of action. And no more mining; it is just too dangerous."

"But what if we need more gold coins next year, for tax day?" Roth asked. "We still have several pounds of raw ore hidden."

"Leave that to me," I said firmly. "I'll take charge of the ore. When the time comes, I'll have it converted into proper coins that not even a shifter can tell from the mages' gold. I have certain...connections who will be able to assist." They did not need to know I could easily accomplish that feat. During my long civil service career, I had created all too many coins myself, and was still perfectly able to do so.

"Fair enough," Marris said. He stood up from the log he'd been sitting on. "That's not for another year, anyway. Let's stop dwelling on such serious topics and go have some fun. How about we head to the tavern and play a few rounds of poker?"

We saddled up our horses, then headed back through the

woods and into town. On the way, we passed by my farm. "Your garden sure is thriving," Cobil said, admiring the rows of vegetables, their shoots and stalks tall and green. "I don't even see any signs of rabbits nibbling."

"You are welcome to help yourself to some of the vegetables while I'm away," I offered.

"Are you really doing this all by yourself?" Marris asked. "I thought you didn't have a lot of farming experience. You must have a green thumb."

"I'm learning," I said, smiling a little. I'd been making heavy use of the agricultural spells I'd memorized long ago, keeping the vermin away and coaxing the plants to grow faster. Without any books to study, I had far too much time on my hands, and I'd resorted to practicing all the household and farming spells I knew.

It's a good thing I have a first-rate memory for spells, I thought as we continued. It had certainly come in handy during Mina's performances, and I had no doubt we would have need of it again in Innarta.

7

FENRIS

After several enjoyable hours of beer and card games in the common room of Abbsville's only inn, Marris and his friends finally decided to head home. I bid the three of them goodnight, staying behind to pay the bill and chat with Julon, the innkeeper. He had become friendlier after the incident with Roor—apparently, he admired me for being able to lift the heavy farmer and throw him across the room with one arm, though it was not a great feat for a shifter. That I'd paid for the damages even though the fight hadn't been my fault had also improved his opinion of me.

"I think you're doing a wonderful thing, keeping an eye out on those three," he said as I finished my beer. "They're good men, but still young and a little too ready to get into trouble."

"They just need to direct all that youthful energy on a worthwhile goal," I said, smiling. I had no doubt the innkeeper knew more than he let on. "Marris has been very welcoming to me since I first arrived, as has his whole family. I am glad to get on well with my nearest neighbors."

I was just about to take my leave when the door opened and

Constable Foggart rushed in, looking harried. The hairs on the back of my neck stood up—he smelled of sweat and worry, and the way his eyes swept the room told me he was looking for someone.

"Evening, Julon, Mr. Shelton," the constable said, coming up to the bar. He glanced around one more time at the few patrons lingering over their drinks, then quietly said, "Is Marris Dolan still here?"

"He just left," I said in an equally low voice. "What is the matter, Constable?"

The constable leaned in. "An agent from the Mages Guild is in town," he whispered, "flashing about a pretty accurate sketch of Marris and asking where he can be found. Some idiot already identified Marris, and the mage is getting a horse now to go out to the Dolan farm. I've promised to show him the way there, but I'm going to take the long way around to buy Marris some time. Someone needs to warn him."

"I'll take care of it." Urgency filled my veins, and I raced out of the inn. My stallion was waiting at the post where I'd left him, ready to go, and I swung myself in the saddle and urged him into a hard gallop. Roundabout way or not, we did not have much time until the mage arrived at Marris's farm—I had to get there first.

There was just enough moonlight through the cloud cover to make out the unpaved road, and I was able to reach the Dolan farm in a matter of minutes. Heart thundering in my ears, I launched off my horse before he had stopped moving completely. I hit the ground running and threw open the door, not bothering to knock.

"Fenris!" Marris jumped to his feet—he'd been sitting on the couch, looking at a book with his sister Dana. "What's going on?"

"An agent from the Mages Guild is here to arrest you." I grabbed Marris by his elbow and hauled him away from the couch. "Quick, you must pack a bag now. We have to leave."

"Arrest Marris?" Mrs. Dolan and Dana cried at the same time.

"For what?" his mother demanded.

"I will explain it to you while he packs." I shoved Marris toward the hallway. "*Go.*"

Marris's two brothers rushed into the room to see what the commotion was about, and I explained the situation to the family as concisely as possible. Marris's mother was furious, but her fear for her son outweighed her anger at his reckless activities. She barked an order for her youngest son to saddle Marris's horse and for her daughter to pack some provisions.

"Okay," Marris panted as he rushed back into the room, a backpack slung over his shoulder. He was dressed head to toe in black, and I nodded in approval—the harder it was for him to be seen, the better.

"I don't know what kind of trouble you've gotten yourself into, Marris Dolan," his mother said fiercely, "but if you get yourself killed, I will bring you back from the dead so I can spank you myself!"

Marris laughed, the sound strained, and pulled his mother into a hug. "I'm sorry, Ma," he said. "But I'll be fine, thanks to Fenris's timely warning."

"You'd better be," Dana said as she handed Marris a bundle of food wrapped in wax paper. She hugged him tightly, tears in her eyes. "You only just came back, Marris. You can't go away again."

"I have to," Marris said gently. "But it won't be for long."

"We'll deny everything," his brother Roglar, a sturdy twenty-year-old, said as Marris pulled away from his sister. "And do our best to stall for as long as possible. We'll tell them you're on a business trip on the East Coast." He clasped Marris in a brief hug. "Now get going."

Not wasting time with more goodbyes, Marris and I ran out of the house and jumped into our saddles. We urged the horses into a swift gallop, racing across the farm and out through the back gate in case the mage was already approaching from the front. My heart pounded in time with the horses' galloping hooves, and I could not help thinking back to my own flight from Nebara all those years ago.

What I was doing tonight was hardly "lying low," which was my whole reason for settling in this remote place. It was one thing to trick a tax inspector, quite another thing to aid and abet Marris when I was a fugitive myself.

But it simply was not in my nature to be a bystander when someone needed me. Marris might have broken the law, but he certainly did not deserve to be punished when he had only been trying to help.

Once we were well away from the farm, we finally let our horses walk. My stallion was particularly winded after I'd pushed him hard twice in one evening. I gratefully patted his sweaty neck and resolved to spoil him with treats as soon as we got home.

"Thank you," Marris said quietly as the grass rustled about us. "You didn't have to do that."

"Of course I did. I couldn't leave you at the mercy of that mage. He would have you hanged, and then where would your family be?"

Marris let out a disgusted sigh. "I can't believe I'm running away," he said, shaking his head. "I wish I'd had a chance to tell Barrla goodbye, at least. Will you tell her I'm sorry for breaking our date? You can tell her the truth about what happened—she won't rat me out, and I want her to know I didn't stand her up on purpose."

"I will." I wasn't relishing the prospect of having that conversation, but neither did Barrla deserve to worry needlessly or think herself forgotten. "In the meantime, let's talk about getting you to safety."

"But what does that mean?" Marris threw up his hands. "I can't just wander from town to town, wasting money while my family suffers without me. I need to do something useful, preferably something that will allow me to bring back some coin when it is safe for me to return home."

"While I don't advise making hasty decisions, there are many paths in life beyond farming, and you are still young enough to start another career. It will be difficult, but your family will get on without you for the next few months—your siblings are old enough, and I will give them a break on the rent if need be."

Marris was silent for a long moment. "You are a better friend than I deserve," he said quietly. "Thank you."

I smiled. "If you truly want to keep busy, there is a mission of sorts I could give you. I've been meaning to do this sooner, but it has been difficult to find someone I can trust."

"Oh?" Marris sounded intrigued. "What sort of mission?"

"I have left a trunk of books in Osero that I need here," I told him. "They are waiting to be picked up at an inn by a 'Mr. Sarman.' If you could go and retrieve them for me, it would be an immense help."

"Seems simple enough."

"Most of the books in the box are forbidden for non-mages to possess," I warned, not mentioning that several of them were unique and quite valuable. "My late uncle, who was a mage, willed them to me. I wish to keep them for sentimental reasons. Above all, you must make certain that no one is watching when you claim the box or follows you back to Abbsville. There is a certain mage out there who would be absolutely delighted to find out I settled here, and it would spell my doom if he were to find out. If you find that the trunk is under surveillance, leave it there and come straight back to report to me."

"Sounds like a challenge." Marris's eyes sparkled—as I expected, he perked right up at the thought of danger. "A mage enemy, eh? You must have lived quite an exciting life."

"There shouldn't be all that much danger," I said wryly, hoping I was right. "It has been many months since he has looked for me, and I have been very careful to hide my trail. Nobody in Osero should be able to connect you and me, so just play dumb if necessary."

"I'm sure I can get the box back to you, no problem," Marris said. He eyed me speculatively, as if he knew there was much more to this story, but thankfully he did not press. "If anyone in authority should try to check the box, I can just pretend to be an agent for the mage owner. Besides, I've learned enough during my time in the Resistance to be able to spot and evade pursuit."

"Very well." I tugged open the money pouch hanging from my belt, then pressed a handful of coins into Marris's palm. "For the journey."

"Thanks." Marris hesitated. "You don't really have to give me money—I still have former comrades-in-arms across the Federation. We help each other out in emergencies. In fact, I'll probably touch base with some of them and see what they're up to while I'm out. If any issues come up, I'll send you a message under the name 'Richiar.'"

"Consider it an advance payment for your time and trouble," I insisted. "And should you return before me, keep the box and hide it securely until I come back."

"Will do."

I traveled with Marris another few miles. Once the lights of the next village became visible in the distance, I bid him farewell and headed back to Abbsville. It seemed Mina and I were not the only ones going on a perilous journey, I mused darkly. I could only hope that we all came back in one piece.

8

MINA

"Well, that wasn't so bad," I said as Fenris and I lounged in comfortable leather chairs in the Deros Airport's waiting room. We'd already completed the first leg of our flight and were waiting for our connection further south to Haralis. "My stomach lurched a bit with nerves when we took off, but once we were actually floating in the air, the flight was quite pleasant."

"I told you it would be." Fenris lightly rubbed my shoulder—his arm was around me and I was leaning lightly against his chest, enjoying the sound of his heartbeat. "Expensive, but worth it."

I'll say. The company charged three gold coins for a two-way trip from Watawis to Innarta, but so far, the journey by air had been far more comfortable than traveling in a cramped steambus, not to mention much faster. With less than three weeks to go until I irrevocably lost my inheritance, I could hardly afford to waste even a single day. I had to get to Haralis before my relatives sold off my estate.

"I hope the cat is all right," I said, chewing on my bottom lip. I had dropped him off with Barrla the previous night. He'd seemed very reluctant when I'd first taken him out of the cage at her house.

"He appeared to warm up to Barrla just fine when you introduced the two of them," Fenris said. "I'm sure by the time you come back the two of them will be inseparable."

I smiled—it would be good if the cat found a permanent home. In the general store belonging to Barrla's family, there would never be any shortage of food. With my future so uncertain, I could hardly commit to taking on a pet, which was ironic since I was a veterinarian by trade.

Furthermore, with Roor and his mother accusing me of witchcraft, and the attention I was getting from the Mages Guild, it was only a matter of time until the truth about my identity was revealed. Sooner or later, people would connect my too-youthful looks, and the way I was able to miraculously cure animals at death's door, with Mrs. Roor's accusations.

Oh well. You were never meant to spend the rest of your life in Abbsville, anyway.

"Ladies and gentlemen," a staff member announced over the loudspeaker, "we regret to inform you that the flight to Haralis is delayed due to inclement weather. We shall inform you as soon as a new departure time is established."

I groaned. "Figures." While the airport was nice enough, with comfortable seating and a coffee stand just a few feet from us selling pastries and beverages, I was not looking forward to waiting here for the next few hours.

"Don't fret," Fenris said. "We can use the time to double-check our plans, see if we missed anything."

I held in a sigh—we had gone over our strategy several times. But considering what was at stake, there was no harm in doing so again. "I'm Tamina Marton," I recited, "and must remember to use my own name at all times." Not that it would be difficult—I'd been going by Mina since I was a child. I would just have to be careful not to sign anything under the alias I'd been using for so long.

"You will be Yoron ar'Tarnis, an elderly mage from the Central Continent who settled in the Federation about two centuries ago," I continued. "You were a beau of my late grandmother, and I went to find you after I fled from my dreadful cousin. Seeing me so distressed, and because I reminded you of your long-lost love, you took me in out of the generosity of your heart." I pressed a hand to my chest in dramatic flair.

Fenris's lips twitched. "And having heard you are about to be declared dead and your inheritance dispersed, we have returned to claim your name and your rightful place in society."

I frowned. "Now that I think about it, some people might not be convinced of your good intentions. They will gossip about us despite the significant age difference, you know."

Fenris shrugged. "I will do my best to behave as an eccentric old mage, no longer interested in a pretty young thing like you. It is true some mages are frisky until they are well into old age, but those who are still interested in dalliances generally use glamour to make themselves appear young and attractive. By showing up with white hair and a grizzled face, I will signal to all and sundry that I am beyond such carnal pursuits, and am only interested in scholarship and esoteric matters." His voice was prim, but a wry smile fleetingly crossed his face. "Believe me, that role will not be hard to maintain. I have had plenty of practice."

I nodded. That was not unusual—mages lived for centuries. After a time, most of them lost their taste for human passions. "Does that happen to shifters?" I asked. "They live quite long as well—do they eventually grow out of lust?"

"No," Fenris said. "Judging by my own experience, shifters are much more virile and alive than either humans or mages— they feel the full range of emotions and urges at any age, and far more strongly. That is why they have such a reputation for being emotional and impulsive."

I arched a brow at that. "I would never use either of those words to categorize *you*, yet you are a shifter."

Fenris inclined his head. "I am not the typical shifter," he admitted. "Most shifters would not have decided to settle in a human town, away from their own kind."

Indeed, I thought, but did not press the point—our relationship was still new. I had to have faith that Fenris would eventually tell me more about his mysterious past. "Would Yoron ar'Tarnis, the kindly old mage, not have acted as my master?" I asked. "And therefore, I would be expected to have finished my apprenticeship?"

Fenris shook his head. "A formal apprenticeship requires the consent of your guardians. For obvious reasons, we could not obtain that. We will be vague about how much magic you have learned, and we should not claim that you are a trained mage or I am your master."

"Maybe we should say I've only come to you in the last two years or so, when we met by chance," I suggested, "and that I had been wandering around among humans. That way, you will not look bad for not giving me much training."

Fenris smiled. "That is an excellent idea. I will introduce myself as your unofficial guardian, and we'll call the Guild upon our arrival and ask for an audience with the Chief Mage. The Chief Mage of Innarta has a good reputation. Chances are he will give you a fair hearing. With any luck, you'll be assigned to a different guardian for the remaining fourteen months until you reach your majority."

I grimaced. "One can only hope." I was not looking forward to having to subjugate myself to some cranky old mage, and I was especially not thrilled about the inevitable confrontation with my relatives. If push came to shove, I'd rather run away again than submit to them as my legal guardians. It was hard enough being their ward when I was fifteen—at twenty-eight, I would not be able to stomach them.

If I'd been given the chance to do an apprenticeship, I might have already completed it by now, rendering this entire issue moot, as mages who completed an apprenticeship were automatically considered to be of age. But if that had happened, I never would have learned how to survive independent of my family, or met Fenris, for that matter.

"It would be best not to mention that I live in the state of Watawis," I decided, "or that I am a trained veterinarian. That way, if things go wrong, we can still retreat to Abbsville."

"That would be prudent," Fenris agreed. "Though it will hopefully not come to that."

"And what if I should be forced to stay with a new guardian in Innarta? Or if they assign me to a mage for my apprenticeship?" I asked. "What will become of our relationship? Will you return to Abbsville without me?" My stomach dropped—I had not truly considered that outcome, yet it was the most logical one, now that I thought about it.

"I don't want to lose you," I murmured, lowering my lashes. My voice was so low that a normal man would not have caught it, but Fenris's expression softened with understanding. He brushed a kiss across my forehead and took my hand in his.

"I am sure we can get someone to watch my property here, or I can sell it," he said against my skin. "In the best-case scenario, I would convince the Chief Mage to allow me to be your new guardian, and we could go back to Abbsville together. But no matter what, I won't leave you, Mina. You won't have to face this alone."

9

MINA

W e arrived in Haralis the following afternoon, Fenris already in his old-mage guise. Once our feet touched the ground, we were immediately whisked off by steamcar to the Black Horse, the luxurious hotel I had advised Fenris to book. By the time I flung myself onto the four-poster bed in my opulent room, I wanted nothing more than to sink into the fluffy white pillows and sleep the rest of the afternoon away. Preferably not alone.

But we had work to do, and Fenris only allowed me a few minutes' rest while he called the Guild to request an interview with the Chief Mage. Once that was done, we went back out to shop for a more suitable wardrobe, since we had not had time to do so in Willowdale. Fenris chose some dark-colored robes, and I bought several silk blouses and two suits that looked crisp and business-like—the sort of outfits a young human lawyer or accountant might wear. The clothing made me look older, more sophisticated. Though it wasn't the same as showing up in mage robes, they should still make a good impression. Hopefully, they would suggest to the Chief Mage that I was a responsible adult rather than a runaway minor.

"What do you think?" Fenris asked in a gruff, slightly warbling voice as he came through the adjoining door of our rooms early the next day. I was still getting used to his new appearance as a tall, lean mage with white hair and bushy brows. He wore a set of blue-gray robes and sported a long nose jutting out from a faintly lined face.

"You look like a dignified elder." I reached up to straighten his robes. "The perfect person to be my guardian. My grandmother probably would have fancied you, actually," I added with a grin.

"Excellent." Fenris grinned back, the look quite uncharacteristic for the type of mage he was impersonating. His eyes—a penetrating blue in this guise—swept over me, and he nodded in satisfaction. "You look perfect."

I reached a hand up to touch my hair, which I'd pulled back into a bun high atop my head. Turning toward the mirror, I smoothed the lapels of my dark blue suit one last time. The peach blouse looked good with it, and the black shoes peeking out from beneath the hem of my pants were shiny. Pearls gleamed at my ears and throat, and I shook my head a little.

"This does not look like me at all."

Fenris put a hand on my shoulder. "You're playing a part," he said gently. "Today, this *is* you."

I nodded and brushed off the feeling of unease. Over recent days, it had occurred to me that while I was legally Tamina Marton, my days of exile had turned me into someone else. If my grandmother had not died when I was fourteen, I would be wearing a full set of mage robes by now, my apprenticeship complete. I probably would have obtained some prestigious position at the Guild—my grandmother had been very influential. I might even be the Haralis version of Clostina.

Instead, I'd spent years studying to become a small-town veterinarian, with none of the manners or characteristics a mage of my status should display. Being Tamina Marton again really did feel like playing a part. Once I claimed my inheritance, I would need to decide whether I wanted to continue to play it, or if I needed to refashion Tamina into someone I would prefer to be.

With those thoughts still spinning about in my head, Fenris and I departed for the Mages Guild. I had never been in the palace myself, but I had driven past it a few times. It looked the same as I remembered—a towering edifice of cream stone and clay tile standing proud against the cloudless blue sky. The gardens around it were in full bloom, bursting with riotous color. When I took in a breath, the fragrant scents of summer flowers filled my nose. A brilliantly blue butterfly fluttered past, then rested for a moment on the rim of a marble fountain. I took a moment to admire it before we continued.

But even butterflies and sweet-smelling gardens could not soothe my nerves completely, and my palms grew clammy as we stepped inside the palace. Vaulted ceilings towered around us as we crossed the amber-colored tile floor, and the furnishings around us whispered of Innarta's wealth. It was one of the most prosperous states in the Federation, with the largest port on the East Coast.

We checked in with the mage receptionist in the lobby, who directed us to a waiting room nearby, promising we would soon be attended to. As we sat in the stiff upholstered chairs, I noticed that even though Fenris kept a bored expression on his face, he seemed tense. I much preferred his shifter looks, I reflected as I studied him, even if he was taller and more imposing now.

A mage in pale green robes appeared only a few minutes later and led us up broad marble steps covered with red velvet carpeting to an interview room on the second floor that looked rather like a parlor where one might serve tea. Indeed, a tea tray was laid out on the coffee table with a platter of cookies. I was too nervous to touch anything, and neither did Fenris.

After a few more minutes of waiting on the fine, plush couches, the door opened and a handsome blond mage entered. He looked to be in his thirties, but if this was the Chief Mage, he was probably much older. Few mages used their natural, unadorned faces past the blush of youth. He was followed by a beautiful dark-haired woman in stunning pink robes shot through with gold, and the staffer who had led us there earlier.

As Fenris caught sight of the female mage, he stiffened almost imperceptibly. If I had not been so attuned to his reactions by now, I would have missed it. As it was, I had to restrain myself from glancing curiously between the two.

"Miss Tamina Marton and Mr. Yoron ar'Tarnis," the staffer said with a bow, then withdrew.

"Good afternoon." The Chief Mage gestured to the chairs across from him, and we sat. "I am Zaran Mallas, Chief Mage of Innarta, and this is my Finance Secretary, Gelisia Dorax."

"Pleased to meet you," Miss Dorax purred, assessing me with her dark gaze. I fought the urge to squirm. "I hear you are a long-lost heiress seeking to reclaim your identity and your estate?"

I sat up straighter. "I am the daughter of Soran and Monissa Marton," I confirmed, addressing the Chief Mage. Something about the Finance Secretary rubbed me the wrong way, and it wasn't just the fact that she was sizing me up as if I were prey. Did she and Fenris know each other? Had they once been lovers?

I pushed aside an absurd flash of jealousy at the idea, forcing myself to block out Miss Dorax. "If you search the papers, you'll probably find my name easily enough—I left Innarta nearly thirteen years ago."

"The name does ring a bell." The Chief Mage frowned. "If

you are indeed this missing heiress, then why did you leave your guardians and stay away all these years? Why did you come back now?"

"I was unaware of the thirteen-year statute until very recently," I said calmly, even as my heart began to beat faster beneath the pressure of his dispassionate gaze. "I ran away when I was fifteen because my cousin Vanley was constantly harassing me, and my aunt and uncle refused to listen to my pleas for help. If I had stayed there much longer, I no doubt would have been raped, perhaps even killed." Chills raced across my skin at the memory of Vanley's hands on me, and I swallowed. "After the callous way my relatives treated me, it would be profoundly unjust for them to steal my inheritance as well, so I have come back to claim it."

"And where have you been all these years?" Miss Dorax challenged, a skeptical look in her eyes. "For a young girl alone in the world, one shudders to think of all that you might have endured. Have you been living with Mr. ar'Tarnis for the past thirteen years?" She made it sound like something scandalous, and I bristled.

"Tamina has only been staying with me for the past two and a half years," Fenris said mildly, cutting in. Whatever reaction he'd felt when he'd seen Miss Dorax had completely disappeared—there was only a cool aloofness in his eyes. "She spent the previous decade on the Central Continent, and we happened to run into each other at a social event where she was working on the staff. I knew and admired her grandmother long ago, and the resemblance between them was too uncanny to not remark on. Once I heard her dreadful story, I could hardly allow her to continue scraping by with manual labor as she has done for most of her youth. I took her in, as any decent mage would do."

"That is very admirable of you," the Chief Mage said dryly.

He did not sound completely convinced by Fenris's dramatic story. "But you really should have sent her back home to Innarta. It does not do to have a minor citizen of the Federation skulking around illegally in another country, presumably under a false name with false papers." He gave me a stern look.

"Well, I am back now," I said, "and anyway, I am hardly a child anymore, even if I am technically still a minor. If I had been allowed to complete the apprenticeship my grandmother had arranged, which my aunt and uncle put off continuously under one pretext or another, I would already be a full mage and enjoying my majority."

"True enough," the Chief Mage agreed. He sat back on the couch and regarded me with a speculative look. "If you grew up here in Haralis, Miss Marton, do you know what a Murmuzel is?"

I had to smile at the memory. "I certainly do. It is the local name of those cute little rodents that live on the trees near the riverbanks. With red stripes and bushy ears. I used to feed them peanuts."

"And do you remember why our schools are closed on October sixth?"

"It is the day the first settlers led by Orkon Trulian reached the site of present-day Haralis," I said. This was something every child in the state would know. I added, "He is one of my remote ancestors, via his daughter Tridaris." It was actually true, and could be checked by any genealogist.

"You do seem to be a native of Haralis," the Chief Mage admitted. "Not many people outside of Innarta would know these details."

"Your aunt and uncle are both prominent members of Haralis society," Miss Dorax said, still eyeing me with suspicion. "With such a large fortune in question—one of the biggest in the state, I believe—it is important your identity be proven beyond doubt, not just by answering a few questions about the area."

I lifted my chin at the challenging undercurrent in her voice. "I am willing to describe any room in my former home, or answer any questions about my family and my previous history. But I doubt that will be necessary—Mr. Ransome, my late grandmother's lawyer, should recognize me easily. I may be older, but I have not changed so much that he will not be able to identify me. I also had a Loranian tutor during the last year of my grandmother's life who was preparing me for my apprenticeship, and a few of my childhood friends from school should still be around."

"That all sounds quite reasonable," the Chief Mage said. Miss Dorax said nothing, her expression unreadable, and I had to wonder what her motivation was. Was she merely suspicious by nature, or did she have an active reason to deny me my inheritance?

"We must look more deeply into the situation," the Chief Mage announced. "Miss Dorax, as Finance Secretary, this matter is within your purview. I hereby charge you with the task of investigating Miss Marton's claim. Please interview all concerned parties and report to me with your findings within the week. I will call everyone together at that time, then make a ruling depending on what you have discovered."

"Very well," Gelisia said. "It should be no trouble at all to uncover the truth." Her eyes gleamed as she studied me again. "Where are you staying?"

"The Black Horse," I said coolly. "You may call on me there whenever you like."

"I will do so tomorrow."

Dismissed, Fenris and I took our leave. As we stepped out into the sunshine, a heavy burden seemed to fall from my shoulders. We'd successfully made it over the first hurdle. All that remained was convincing Miss Dorax that my claim was legitimate. I hoped that I was wrong about my initial impression of her, and that she would be less antagonistic during our next interview.

But as we climbed into one of the steamcabs waiting at the curb, my leaden gut and Fenris's grave face told me otherwise. My intuition was rarely wrong, and I had a feeling the beautiful Finance Secretary was about to bring us trouble.

10

FENRIS

Mina was quiet on the way back, and I was grateful for the silence. As the steamcar rumbled along the cobbled streets, I glared out the window, barely registering the scenery that passed by. Haralis was a beautiful coastal city. It was in many ways reminiscent of Solantha, though the architecture had a distinctly different style, but I did not appreciate it right now. All I could see was Gelisia Dorax's face and the barely concealed greed in her eyes as she'd gazed upon Mina. I could practically hear the gears in her head turning, and knew her wicked mind was concocting some dastardly scheme to turn Mina's situation to her own advantage.

It had been a miracle I'd managed to keep my composure at all. Gelisia's malice and ambition had cost me my career, and very nearly my life, when she'd turned traitor on me without any warning. Thankfully, she would not recognize me in this guise, nor would she recognize me even if I appeared in my natural form. She had known me as Polar ar'Tollis, not Fenris the shifter. As far as she knew, I was still at large, or presumed dead.

It would do me no good to be angry at Gelisia now, I decided.

The past was the past, and I had to focus on Mina. There was no reason Gelisia would suspect me of anything.

You've underestimated her before, I told myself, *and that did not end well for you.*

That was true enough. I would have to be extra careful now that she was a player in this dangerous game. It was interesting that she'd ended up as Finance Secretary again, the same position she had held under me. I supposed she had somehow managed to leverage her resume—I had not thought to inquire what had become of her after I'd settled in Solantha with Iannis.

"Are you all right?" Mina touched my arm, drawing me away from my troubled thoughts. "You seem quite put out."

I nodded. *"It would be best to discuss any sensitive subjects in silence,"* I reminded her—the driver could overhear us.

"You knew that dark-haired woman, didn't you?" Mina asked pointedly, and I blinked. The tone in her voice...it almost sounded jealous. *"She is very beautiful and sophisticated."*

"She is a viper, and you must remain on guard at all times," I warned. It was impossible for me to see Gelisia as beautiful anymore—every time I thought about her, I remembered the smug look on her face as she played that magical recording of my prison raid to Garrett Toring, who had been the Federal Secretary of Justice at the time. *"She is ruled by nothing but cold ambition and will stab you in the back if she thinks it will help her get what she's after. If she pretends to befriend you, it will be for ulterior motives."*

Mina arched a brow. *"I got the impression that she was not a nice woman, but how do you know all this? You sound like you've clashed with her before."* Her tone was rife with curiosity.

"Indeed, I've come across her before," I said vaguely, unwilling to delve further into the subject. I did not want to burden Mina with the full knowledge of my past—once she knew who I was and where I came from, she would not be able to deny anything

should I be arrested, and might even be in danger of becoming an accessory after the fact.

"It was not a happy experience." A vast understatement. *"We must ensure she does not get a shred of information that she could use to turn the case against you. The less we have to deal with her, the better."*

Mina tried to question me a bit more about Gelisia, but I refused to divulge more information. Eventually, she huffed. *"Well, at least you make an impressively wise ancient mage,"* she said. *"Though I do wish you could escort me in your normal guise. You are much more handsome as Fenris."*

I smiled at that, resisting the urge to kiss her brow. I wondered what she would have thought of Polar. The old mage whose guise I wore did not resemble me when I had been a mage, except in stature, which was just as well given my unexpected encounter with Gelisia.

We got off the streetcar and entered a restaurant the hotel's concierge had recommended for an early dinner. It was still fairly empty before sunset, so we were able to get a window table with an excellent view of the city without having a reservation. As we sipped wine and admired the view of the sparkling ocean beyond the city skyline, we switched to verbal communication and discussed our plans for the next day.

"We have an appointment tomorrow at ten with Mr. Ransome," I said. "When I called earlier, he was quite eager to meet me as the fictitious buyer for your mansion. I imagine he will be very surprised when the heiress he is trying to declare legally dead shows up instead."

Mina smiled. "Part of me is looking forward to his reaction," she admitted. "From the two letters, he seemed pretty sure I was never coming back. I must get him to tell us exactly why he was so certain of my demise, and what my aunt and uncle told him after I disappeared." Her brow creased, her expression turning somber. "I wonder if they even searched for me at all."

"They likely did, for appearances' sake," I said, "but probably not very far, or very thoroughly. If your aunt and uncle truly did not care for you, they might have been secretly relieved when you disappeared."

Mina's eyes briefly shone with tears, and I immediately regretted my tactless comment. But she blinked them away, regaining her composure. "I was terrified of pursuit that first year," she said quietly, tracing the rim of her glass with her fore-finger. "I kept my head down as much as I could, fearing they were hunting me down and would drag me back. If I had known they wouldn't even bother looking for me outside Innarta, my life would have been much easier." Her voice was thick with irony.

"We don't know yet what they did. We ought to check with the local paper and see if your disappearance was, in fact, in the news," I suggested. "Since the Chief Mage recognized your name, there was probably some report. We should verify how they recounted the story. A young, pretty heiress disappearing in the middle of the night should have made for a juicy morning read or two, but perhaps it was hushed up for whatever reason."

Our food arrived, and we lapsed into silence as we enjoyed the gourmet fare—roast duckling and lamb. The meat was quite tender, but the quantity was not nearly enough for a shifter with my appetite, so I ended up ordering a second plate. The server eyed me with amazement when I then proceeded to order dessert—clearly, he was not used to old mages tucking away food as though they were starving young men. I would have thought it strange, too, in his position.

"Well, well," Gelisia's voice sounded from behind me, and my shoulders tightened. Turning in my seat, I hid a grimace when I saw her winding her way through the tables toward us.

"Imagine the two of you dining in my favorite restaurant! What a pleasant surprise."

"Miss Dorax." Mina gave her a superficial smile. "How nice to see you again so soon. Would you like to join us?"

"Indeed I would." Gelisia pulled up a chair and sat down between Mina and me, far too close for my comfort. Her cloying perfume stung my nostrils, and I had to fight back the urge to sneeze. How had I ever found this witch attractive?

Gelisia ordered a cocktail from the server, then settled back in her chair with a feline smile. "I planned to interview you tomorrow, but since you're here, I might as well use the occasion to ask a few questions that came to me after you left. You don't mind, do you?"

"Not at all," Mina said, and I had to admire her unruffled composure. I didn't even scent a hint of fear from her. "Anything to help the case along."

"I love how cooperative you are," Gelisia cooed. "I'm sorry if I came across as skeptical earlier—but as Finance Secretary, it is my job to be suspicious of anyone trying to claim substantial amounts of money, especially inheritances. I'm sure we'll have this all sorted out soon enough."

Mina smiled. "I don't mind you doing your job," she said as she forked up a bite of chocolate cake. "Now, what questions do you have for me?"

Gelisia spent the next few minutes asking about Mina's past —where she went to school, how long she had lived with her grandmother, and where she had gone while she was living abroad. Mina answered the questions calmly and concisely, and I did my best to remain as unobtrusive as possible even as my gut knotted with tension.

"It was very gallant of you to take Miss Marton in the way you did," Gelisia purred after Mina told her how we had met by chance. Gelisia turned her seductive gaze on me, and I barely suppressed a grimace when she laid her hand on my forearm. "I'm certain Tamina did not want for anything while she was in your care." Her fingers subtly brushed against the gold threading of my robe, and I had no doubt she was sizing up my wealth and stature. She might have even dug into my assumed family's history already.

"It was the least I could do," I said, then turned the conversation back on her. I did not like all these probing questions—she seemed friendly enough, but I suspected she was hunting for a weakness in Mina's armor, anything about her story that did not add up. "You seem quite young to be a Finance Secretary, Miss Dorax. How long have you been working here at the Innarta Mages Guild?"

"Oh, a few years now." Gelisia waved a manicured hand. "I started as deputy, but I have a very good head for finances and was promoted within six months."

"Six months? That's impressive," I said, injecting an admiring note in my voice. In reality, I was quite put out—I'd expected a larger setback in her career. The Lady knew she deserved it, after what she'd done to me. Did she move to Innarta because the Chief Mage, like me, was unmarried? I wondered if she was waiting for the chance to blackmail him—I had no doubt she was up to her old tricks.

Across the table, Mina eyed the two of us—there was a distinctly annoyed look on her face, and I felt a flash of amusement at her jealousy. I would have to reassure her when we were alone that she had nothing to fear—there was no force in Recca that could compel me to fall for Gelisia's wiles a second time.

"It is a pity you are not yet a full mage," Gelisia said, turning back to Mina. "I am surprised you are as behind on your studies as you claim—*I* graduated when I was only twenty-three."

"Well, that is very fortunate for you," Mina said coolly, narrowing her eyes. "Perhaps I would have graduated early, too, if I had been lucky enough to have supportive guardians and a real master to teach me."

Gelisia stiffened at the censure in Mina's voice. "I would take care with the tone you use around me," she said. "Whether you recover your fortune or not is entirely dependent on keeping my favor."

"Is that so?" I said as a flash of anger ignited in my veins. "Surely you will report the truth, whatever you find it to be, and the Chief Mage will be the one who makes the ruling."

Gelisia shrugged. "Certainly. But there are many ways to shade the truth, and we can talk later how to ensure I will make it favorable for your ward here." She gave Mina another cat-like smile. Mina merely stared back, stone-faced.

"I would not dare to try to bias you in any way," I said, refusing to take the bait. It sounded like Gelisia expected me to buy her off, and while that would make Mina's life easier, I refused to fall in with her machinations.

Gelisia frowned. "Well, this has been fun, but I really must be going." She stood, hitching her small handbag on her shoulder. "Enjoy your evening."

Mina and I exchanged looks of profound relief as Gelisia walked away, and I lifted a hand to signal the waiter.

"She never paid for her cocktail," Mina murmured.

"Typical," I grumbled, and ordered another drink. I felt like I'd just entertained a snake at dinner, and I needed a brandy to wash the sour taste from my mouth.

11

FENRIS

After we'd finished dinner, Mina and I caught a cab back to our hotel room and prepared to settle down for the night. We'd booked two hotel rooms for appearances' sake, but they had an adjoining door. It was not difficult for her to slip into my room after the two of us had entered through our respective doors.

"We definitely can't trust Miss Dorax to make a fair assessment of the case," Mina said in mindspeak. She sat down in the small sofa by the window, looking pensive. *"I will have to keep an eye on her and make sure that she is not twisting the evidence."*

"I would strongly advise you keep your distance," I told her, alarmed at the very idea of Mina tangling with Gelisia. *"She is dangerous, and far more devious than you could ever imagine. It would be much better if you left her to me."*

Mina crossed her arms over her chest. "And just how is it that you know this?" she asked aloud, her eyes gleaming with challenge. "You can't keep stalling forever—if you have information about this woman, you should tell me. I need to know what I am dealing with."

I winced—that was true enough. And it was clear Mina

would not allow me to keep her in the dark about my past forever. She had trusted me enough to confide her painful family problems. If I refused to reciprocate, it would only drive a wedge between us.

"Very well," I conceded. I conjured a privacy bubble around the room to keep anyone outside from overhearing, dropped my mage illusion, and sat down in the chair across from her. "I've indeed met Gelisia in the past, in a different guise than the one I've been wearing today. She was the Finance Secretary in another state and had designs on the Chief Mage's position. I know her to be very crafty and devious, and not above leveraging other people's circumstances to get what she wants. I just so happened to be in her crosshairs. She damaged my reputation severely and forced me to flee the state." That was true enough, though it was a very abbreviated version of what had happened to me.

Mina's eyes were wide. "*She* is the reason you are in hiding?"

"Partly, though mostly I have only myself to blame," I admitted. "Running across her again is most unfortunate, and we must be very careful. I cannot be seen in public as anything but the old mage, and we must keep the curtains drawn whenever we are here at the hotel." That was the first thing I'd done when we returned. "She likes to use animals to spy on her targets, and even uses a magical spell to record from afar what people say and do. We must take every precaution we are not overheard when we discuss anything that could reveal my identity."

Mina nodded, her expression grave. "Should we keep to our rooms while we are here, then?" she asked reluctantly. "So long as we are indoors, and careful, we should be able to avoid her machinations."

I shook my head. "It would not do for us to be holed up in here all day—you need to be out and about, showing your face to as many people as possible. Haralis may be large, but word travels fast, and you are bound to be recognized. It will be more difficult for your relatives to deny your claim if multiple witnesses back you."

"True enough," Mina agreed. "Maybe it would be good if I learned the privacy spell, too."

I spent the next twenty minutes working with Mina on a simpler version of the spell I had used on the room—she was not yet advanced enough to use the same spell I did, but the one I taught her would create a bubble around herself and a person of her choice so the two of them could speak without being overheard. Mina should only need to use it when talking to others—when she was with me, we could use mindspeak.

"Very good," I said as she successfully conjured the bubble for the third time. "I think we can leave off for tonight."

Mina dissipated the bubble with a wave of her hand, then leaned against the wall. Her face was flushed with exertion, but rather than looking tired, her silver-gray eyes were bright. "It is... quite gratifying, being able to channel my powers effectively," she said, pushing a strand of hair away from her face. "I can't tell you enough how much it means to me that you're helping me with this."

"It is my pleasure, I assure you." Entranced by the glow in her face and the way her eyes sparkled, I closed the distance between us so I could cup her cheek. "You are a quick student," I murmured, brushing my thumb across her lower lip. "I have no doubt you will complete your training well before the usual ten years."

Mina's lashes fluttered as she tilted her chin up. "No doubt," she agreed, sliding her arms around my neck. I kissed her, and a growl rumbled from my chest as she pressed her willowy curves against me. The scent of her arousal was already stirring the air, and I breathed it in deeply, along with her lavender and sunshine scent. Her soft mouth was divine. As primal hunger awoke inside me, I teased the seam of her lips with my tongue. She opened for me eagerly, as anxious to taste me as I was her, and I slid my hands beneath her rear to lift her up and carry her to the bed.

In a matter of moments, I'd divested her of her blouse, leaving her upper half bared to my gaze. "Mmm," she moaned as I took one of her dusky nipples into my mouth, gently swirling my tongue around it. She gasped when I bit down, her fingers digging into my shoulders. Another bolt of lust surged through me, making me impossibly hard, and I wanted to be inside her so badly I nearly shredded the rest of her clothes off.

Instead, I used my magic to make them disappear.

"Oh!" Mina's eyes flew wide as she realized what I'd done. Her lips curved into a smile as she ran her hands down my suddenly bare chest. "You'll have to teach me that trick," she said, her hands sliding down to wrap her fingers around me. I groaned as she squeezed gently and then began to stroke the underside of my length with her thumb.

"You're getting quite good at that," I gasped as she continued to pleasure me.

"I would hope so," she said, tangling her free hand in my hair. She kissed me hard as she stroked me, and my body trembled with the urge to take her.

But Mina was not taking any contraceptives—they were hard to come by in Abbsville, she'd explained to me. I couldn't risk impregnating her. Not when there was still the possibility that she might find a more suitable partner, one she could be with openly.

Instead, I let her finish me, saturating myself in the taste and smell of her until she brought me to a roaring climax. And then I crawled down her body and feasted on her until she'd come so many times she was begging for mercy.

12

FENRIS

O nce Mina was gone, I stretched out in my bed, utterly satisfied. How in Recca had I ever been attracted to Gelisia? I wondered as I stared up at the ceiling. Next to Mina's gentle nature, the woman was as fake as a wooden doll. I had been a fool to allow Gelisia to worm her way into my office and take up such a critical position in the Nebara Mages Guild. At least we had never been lovers, despite her blatant invitations. A few dates and kisses were as far as things had gone.

But I am not the only fool, I thought with a spark of wry amusement. The Chief Mage of Innarta had also been taken in by Gelisia's charms, and I had no doubt she was going to make a play for his seat, just as she had done with me. It would be in Mina's and my best interests if I found a way to eliminate her, but there was no easy way to do so without drawing attention to myself, which I could ill afford.

Gelisia would dig into our backgrounds, searching for whatever dirt she could find. That would be difficult with my fictitious overseas background, but there was always a chance she might discover my alias was fake. If that happened, I was in a world of trouble. Mina, on the other hand, would be easier to investigate, but I doubted Gelisia would unearth anything incriminating, unless there was something about Mina's past she had not yet divulged to me.

She'll also likely spy on Mina, I thought, frowning. Mina would have no way of knowing whether Gelisia's familiars were nearby —she could be vigilant and watch out for suspicious animals, but Gelisia was clever and would keep her spies unobtrusive. Wondering if there was any way to repel her, I mentally rifled through my magical repertoire. Unfortunately, some of the more difficult spells that would come in handy in this situation were beyond my current magical strength. I might eventually be able to perform them again—my power had gradually increased in the four years since my transformation—but for now, I would have to stick to less taxing rituals.

I wondered how Sunaya was coping with all the spells I'd given her. It had been a good eight months since I'd gifted her with my knowledge and memories. While she would have had time to start sifting through my memories, there was no way she could have tried out even a fraction of my vast magical repertoire. After an apprenticeship with one of the most accomplished mages in the Federation, I had continued to study and learn spells for well over a century. Some of them were considered long-lost, and I was the only one who'd known them before I passed my knowledge on to Sunaya.

Eventually, I settled on a protection spell, the strongest one I could still manage. Rising from the bed, I sat on the floor, cross-legged, then reached into the magical pocket that hovered just beneath my left elbow and pulled out a lock of Mina's hair I'd taken one night while she'd been sleeping. I felt slightly guilty for taking a piece of her without her knowledge, but I had worried I might someday need it for a tracking spell should something ever happen to her.

It's a good thing I took it, I thought as I pulled out a mother-ofpearl-handled knife. *She'll need all the protection she can get now that Gelisia is in the middle of this mess.*

I sliced the knife along the palm of my left hand, opening a wound deep enough that my shifter abilities would not heal it instantly. I dripped a few drops into a cup, then added the hair and some other ingredients also conveniently located in my magical pocket. Once finished, I held the cup in both hands, then chanted the Loranian spell to power it.

Closing my eyes, I envisioned my magic pouring into the cup, holding a picture of Mina in my mind's eye. The cup hummed with power as I lifted it high, and I opened my eyes just in time to hear the whoosh of flame as the contents ignited. The scent of burning hair and magic stung my nostrils, and I resisted the urge to sneeze as smoky tendrils of power formed in the air. They snaked beneath the adjoining door, where they would bind themselves to Mina while she slept.

A wave of tiredness hit me, and I sat back against the foot of the bed, satisfied all had worked as expected. The protection spell would help keep Mina safe in the event of a magical attack, and to some extent even a physical one, though there were limitations to what it could do. Its protection would last for several weeks. Even if Gelisia weren't meddling in Mina's affairs, the spell was a good idea—her greedy relatives might well try to put Mina out of the picture permanently, especially if they had already spent a significant portion of her fortune.

Once my momentary fatigue had passed, I washed up, then slid into bed to try once again to get some sleep. But I tossed and turned, restless, and it took a moment for me to realize that my blood was still humming. Not with lust, as it had been earlier... but from the pull of the moon.

I got out of bed and pushed back the curtains enough to peek out. Sure enough, the moon was hanging bright and full in the sky, so large it felt like I could reach out and touch it. My fangs lengthened as the moon's silent song pulled at me, and my blood surged in my veins, urging me to change.

I might be unlike normal shifters in some respects, but their innate urges still called to me. I had to get out and run, at least for a little while, or I would be on edge all day tomorrow. And with everything that was going on, I needed my wits about me.

Not bothering to get dressed, I cloaked myself in an illusion spell. Disguised as one of the hotel staff, I silently slipped out the back door and into the alley filled with dumpsters. In the quiet darkness, I allowed the change to take hold of me, enveloping me in a glowing white light as my body morphed into the wolf. I did not know how it felt to other shifters, but for me, the transformation was always quick and painless.

When it was done, I blinked to clear the light from my vision. Once the spots had faded away, my eyes focused easily in the darkness. The stench of the dumpster was nearly unbearable to my wolf's nose—my senses were even stronger as a shifter, my hearing sharper, my night vision better. The sound of a raccoon slinking nearby caught my ears, and I surged forward, letting my wolf take over.

It might be a densely populated, large city, but there was no reason why I could not hunt. And that nearby beach, with its wide expanse of sand and surf, had looked like an excellent place for running.

13

MINA

The next morning, Fenris and I rose bright and early and enjoyed a light breakfast in the hotel's restaurant. Even in his old-mage guise, he looked refreshed and energetic, I observed over my glass of orange juice as he dug into his giant plate of eggs and bacon with a fervor I could never hope to match. Much more relaxed than he had been yesterday.

Lovemaking will do that to a person, I reflected. Indeed, by the time I returned to my own room, I had been so relaxed and sated that I'd fallen asleep the instant my head had hit the pillow. It had been an effort to leave Fenris's bed last night, but even though it was unlikely someone would barge into either of our rooms, we couldn't risk being caught together.

My cheeks warmed as I remembered the way he'd worshipped my body, how he'd kissed and licked nearly every inch of me, places I had never thought I'd feel a man's lips. My toes curled as heat flashed low in my belly, and I moistened my lips with my tongue.

"We are never going to get out of here if you keep thinking about sex," Fenris murmured, raising his gaze to meet mine. His eyes gleamed with a hunger that had nothing to do with the food on his plate. "I can tell, you know." His nostrils flared.

My ears reddened with embarrassment, and I resisted the urge to duck my head. "It isn't my fault you're so good in bed," I said, cutting a piece of buttered toast and lifting it to my lips. "I was simply indulging in some pleasant memories to give myself a boost before our meeting with the lawyer."

Fenris chuckled. "I am glad to be of service," he said wryly, forking up the last of his eggs. "We should get going soon—our meeting is in half an hour."

We paid the tab, then took a cab across town to where Mr. Ransome's office was located. This part of Haralis was mostly filled with brick office buildings and storefronts—the business section of town where professionals rented office space or business owners sold supplies to other companies. The building in question was one of the nicer ones, a narrow, four-story granite structure that towered over the others and no doubt boasted a beautiful view of the city. After consulting the directory, we used the elevator.

"Good morning," the receptionist said as we walked into the tastefully appointed lobby of Mr. Ransome's third-floor office. She had been typing furiously, so I guessed she was also his secretary. "How can I help you?"

"I'm Garton Branis, here to see Mr. Ransome about an estate matter," Fenris said, giving the assumed name he had used for their correspondence. He still wore the old-mage guise, which worked well enough—nobody here knew what Branis was actually supposed to look like.

"Very good. Please, take a seat. Mr. Ransome will be out to see you in a moment."

Contrary to her words, we were kept waiting for nearly fifteen minutes, which was a little annoying. If the Chief Mage could see us within five, surely Mr. Ransome could be as punctual, especially when he thought he was about to make money. But Fenris merely leafed through the coffee-table magazines, looking unconcerned, so I forced myself to do the same.

A large part of my annoyance stemmed from the fact that I wanted to get this over with. But after thirteen years of running from my former life, I could hardly undo it all in one day. I would have to be patient.

"Mr. Ransome will see you now," the secretary announced at last. We stood, and she led us into a larger office through a door behind her desk.

"Good afternoon—" Mr. Ransome began as he rose from his desk, then cut himself off. His eyes widened in astonishment as he took me in, and triumph rose in me as I caught the recognition in his gaze. "Miss..." He stopped himself, seeming to think better of calling me by my name, and I frowned.

"Miss Tamina Marton," I finished for him. "Surely you recognize me still, Mr. Ransome?" He had not changed very much since I last saw him. Unlike most mages, he wore a business suit and tie, and the vest beneath stretched around his portly frame. His walrus mustache was a bit more silver, as was his thick crown of hair, but the spectacles and the keen blue eyes behind them were exactly as I remembered.

Fenris narrowed his eyes, looking as displeased with the lawyer's reaction as I was. Was Mr. Ransome deliberately pretending not to recognize me?

"Yes, yes, of course!" His face brightened as he came around the desk to shake my hand. "You'll have to forgive me, Miss Marton —I did not want to call you by your name in case I was mistaken."

I laughed as I shook his hand. "And why would you think that you were mistaken?"

Mr. Ransome cleared his throat. "Well, you have been missing for nearly thirteen years—everyone said you had drowned in the ocean. You can understand why we would have concluded that, since you never did resurface."

I crossed my arms over my chest, staring at him. *"Drowned?* Why would anyone assume that I'd drowned?" I said. "Nobody actually saw me go into the ocean, did they?" My aunt and uncle's house was quite close to the shore, and I could have easily run for the water, but I hadn't done any such thing.

An uncomfortable look crossed Mr. Ransome's face. "Why don't we sit down so we can talk about this properly?" he said, waving us toward the chairs. "Who is your associate?"

"Yoron ar'Tarnis," Fenris said smoothly. He shook Mr. Ransome's hand. "Miss Marton sought refuge with me in my home on the Central Continent, where she fled after escaping the terrors of her family's household."

"Terrors?" Mr. Ransome's eyebrows winged up. "What in Recca are you talking about?"

"The night I disappeared, I was attacked by my cousin Vanley," I said flatly. I held my emotions in an iron grip as I met Mr. Ransome's gaze—I had no intention of falling to pieces in front of him, even if the damsel-in-distress attitude might be a more effective strategy. I was the heiress of my grandmother's estate, come back to claim what was rightfully mine—not a cowering victim. "He had been harassing me, both emotionally and sexually, since the day I moved in with his parents, and he was threatening to rape me that night. I managed to get away from him using my magic, but I knew I might not be so lucky the next time, so I ran and never looked back. At least until I found out that the bastard and his family were about to inherit my money," I added with a frown.

"That's terrible." Mr. Ransome's face softened into an expression of sympathy. "I had no idea you were suffering such abuse in the Cantorin household. Of course, I did not see you after the funeral...your aunt and uncle said you were still settling in when I asked after you."

"He is telling the truth," Fenris said in mindspeak. *"He did not know what was happening in your house."*

My shoulders sagged a little in relief—so Mr. Ransome had not been involved. "What did my aunt and uncle tell you about that night?" I asked. "Surely Vanley suffered some sort of injury —I left him unconscious that night." I'd been so angry and terrified that I hadn't cared whether he lived or died, though I didn't dare say so to the lawyer.

Mr. Ransome frowned. "They didn't mention that part at all, actually. I presume they either called for a healer or took care of Vanley's injuries themselves rather than risk being questioned about it. Or perhaps he was merely stunned and recovered on his own—you were only fifteen, and he's always been a hardy young man."

I nodded—that was true enough. I'd been so desperate to escape I hadn't bothered to check on Vanley after he'd tumbled down the stairs—it was possible his injuries hadn't been as great as I'd feared.

"Mrs. Cantorin told me you had been moody and depressed over the last few months, to the point they had to repeatedly postpone your apprenticeship. They had thought you were improving, especially since you were venturing out of the house more instead of holing yourself up in your room with grief over your grandmother's death. According to them, you went swimming the night you went missing and never returned. They blamed themselves for not getting you professional help if you were self-destructive, though it was unclear if you had succumbed to an accident or tried to kill yourself."

"I see," I said tightly, anger simmering in my veins. "For the record, it was not my habit to go swimming alone at night, and I certainly never contemplated killing myself." I would not have given Vanley the satisfaction. I had been depressed, certainly, but that had been *because* my aunt and uncle refused to allow me to start my apprenticeship and had kept me trapped in that horrid house instead. That, coupled with Vanley's incessant abuse, was enough to drive anyone mad. "Was any effort made to recover my body?"

"Of course," Mr. Ransome said. "A search was conducted. But as I recall, the enforcers mostly looked for washed-up bodies. They did not post any kind of alert across state lines, in part, I suspect, because your family was anxious to avoid scandal. In retrospect, had we known you did not go into the sea, we would have broadened our search. We were remiss in not doing so in the first place," he admitted.

"Indeed," Fenris said coldly, drawing Mr. Ransome's gaze to him. "Was there no suspicion of foul play at all? Surely you or the enforcers should have at least considered the possibility, since the 'witnesses' to Miss Marton's supposed drowning stood to benefit so greatly from this alleged tragedy."

Mr. Ransome shrugged. "The Enforcers Guild did pursue that line of questioning at first, but the family appeared shocked and saddened by Miss Marton's death, and there was no evidence regarding the abuse Miss Marton speaks of. Eventually, they must have believed them," he speculated. "For my part, even had I felt the slightest suspicion, it would have been highly inappropriate to tarnish the reputation of such a respectable mage family without proof. Especially when their grief was so obvious."

"If they truly were so saddened by my 'passing,'" I said, "then they will be overjoyed once they learn of my return. It is a good thing I have come back—I hear that the statutory thirteen years are about to expire. Since my relatives have not moved into my grandmother's house, I can only imagine they would either rent it out or try to sell it off."

"Yes, we shall soon sort out the disposition of your estate," Mr. Ransome said briskly. "Where exactly are you and your, ah, escort staying? I must inform your aunt and uncle of your whereabouts, since they are still your legal guardians."

A chill shot down my spine, and I clamped down on the fear that tried to take over. *You aren't running anymore*, I reminded myself firmly. "We are staying at the Black Horse."

"Ah, a fine establishment." Mr. Ransome nodded in approval. "I will contact your family today, and I will also advise them to stop the procedure to have you declared dead. It is fortunate you are here now, as it is nearly complete."

"You should be aware that Miss Dorax, the Finance Secretary, is looking into the case," I said. "She will probably stop by today or tomorrow to question you."

Mr. Ransome grimaced, clearly displeased at this news. "She is probably hoping to squeeze more inheritance taxes out of the estate," he grumbled. "But no matter, I will deal with her."

He showed us out with the promise to be in touch as soon as he'd spoken to my family. And as we left, I couldn't help but wonder what it would be like to be a fly on the wall for *that* conversation.

14

MINA

Our next stop was the *Haralis Monitor*, the city's local newspaper. Since it was only a few blocks away and a pleasant day, Fenris and I decided to walk rather than sit on our butts in a steamcab.

As we strolled through the neatly kept avenues shaded by chestnut trees, I found myself more pensive than I had expected to be. Though it had been nearly a decade since I'd left here, I had expected to feel some connection with the city of my birth, now that I was back. But nearly all the buildings and street names were foreign to me—I recognized a few landmarks, but they did not tug at me with recognition. They did not whisper to me of home.

You don't belong here anymore, a voice in my head murmured. *You've changed too much.*

"Are you all right?" Fenris asked, glancing at me with concern. I wondered if my expression was that dour, or if he merely caught a change in my scent—he could read me so easily it was unnerving sometimes.

I sighed deeply. "I just...expected more." I waved a hand to indicate the streets before us. "To be more excited to return. But somehow this feels like a letdown, which is silly." I laughed lightly, shaking my head. "This is far more exciting than Abbsville, isn't it?"

"Perhaps," he said, "but if I were to return to my hometown after so many years of being away, and with bad memories so close to the surface, I, too, would feel uncomfortable."

Uncomfortable. Yes, that was the word to describe the prickling across my skin, the way my gut tightened and my hands grew cold when we'd entered the Mages Guild yesterday. The urgency of it all had kept me from dwelling on it too much, but I'd felt like an outsider, like I didn't fit in. Which was silly, because I was a full-blooded mage, just like any of the others.

Most mages don't become veterinarians. Or live for years disguised as a human in a small town.

Perhaps I'd spent so long in hiding that I'd forgotten what it was like to be a mage. I had still been a teenager when I'd left and hadn't ever received the training that made most mages appear so rigid and controlled. Keeping a handle on one's emotions was essential when wielding powerful magic—the consequences of an unexpected flash of anger could be devastating. Combine that trained reserve with the haughty attitude of the wealthy, and it was little wonder that I didn't fit in.

"Wow," I said as we turned onto another street. The headquarters of the *Haralis Monitor* stood just across from us on the corner, a tall, sparkling glass-and-stone building in green with the name of the paper in large letters above the doors. I'd never actually been here—there hadn't been any reason for me to visit the newspaper. "It's much more modern-looking than I expected."

We stepped inside. A silver-haired woman in her fifties sat behind a reception desk. She wore a white skirt suit that flattered her willowy, elegant frame, and she sat in her chair with such poise and grace that for a moment, I felt a flash of envy. I hoped I looked half as good as that when I finally got old, even if that wasn't for hundreds of years yet.

"Good morning," she said pleasantly, flashing a perfect smile. "How can I help you?"

"My name is Tamina Marton," I said, smiling back. "And this is Mr. ar'Tarnis. We would like to check on a story that would have appeared in your paper not quite thirteen years ago. Is that possible?"

"Yes, we do keep a complete collection of our editions," she said. "Is this for research purposes?"

Fenris smiled at her, and she seemed to thaw a little. "You might say that—background research that is very important for a legal case. We'd appreciate the assistance."

"You will have to sign here before you are admitted," she said, pulling out a guestbook. "And write down where you're staying."

Fenris signed first, in large, round letters very unlike his usual script. As I put pen to paper, I nearly signed the book as Mina Hollin before I remembered I was operating under my birth name now. It was very strange to sign as Tamina Marton, and the resultant signature was a bit sloppy. I would have to practice signing with my legal name now—the sooner I got used to it, the better.

Satisfied, the receptionist gave us instructions to get to the archives, then picked up the phone to call ahead and let them know we would be coming.

The archive clerk was a short, balding man with round spectacles. When he opened the door to admit us, he was vibrating with excitement. "Miss Marton herself, back from the dead!" he exclaimed as he ushered us in. "I remember your story—it was quite the scandal, although quickly hushed up. I'm so glad to see that you did not perish in the waters after all."

"Thank you." I beamed—it was good to see that at least one

person was genuinely happy I was alive. "Can you help me find the editions that referred to my disappearance? I imagine there were more than one."

"It's no trouble at all."

The clerk led us down one of the many corridors of shelves, toward the back of the room. Lining the shelves were huge bound folders filled with slightly yellowing newspaper pages. He selected three of them. They were heavy, but I lifted one easily enough as Fenris and the clerk each took another—all the years I'd spent as a veterinarian, delivering calves and foals, had made me stronger than the average female mage. We carried the folders over to a large table, and the clerk helped us riffle through them and pick out the editions in question.

He looked inclined to hover and chat, but Fenris thanked him. When he pressed a coin into his hand as a tip, the clerk got the message. He disappeared back into the maze of shelves, leaving us to study the papers in peace.

I picked up the earliest edition, published two days after I'd fled, feeling a pang as I studied the title: "Young Heiress Goes Missing—Presumed Drowned." Below was a picture of me, my face still round and soft with youth, and my gut twisted. I was smiling at the camera, a carefree innocence in my eyes as I posed in a chair wearing a fancy dress. My grandmother had that portrait of me taken just a year before she'd passed away—I must have been thirteen.

"Interesting," Fenris said as he read the article over my shoulder. "It appears your aunt actually offered a cash reward for any information about your whereabouts."

I pursed my lips. "That might have just been for show," I said. "I don't suppose she truly cared." But a sliver of doubt niggled at me—perhaps my aunt and uncle truly hadn't known? Reading on, I discovered that Vanley was the one who had witnessed my "midnight swim." He'd claimed to have seen me walking out to the water in the middle of the night from his bedroom, wearing my swimsuit. My lip curled in disdain—if he'd truly caught me running about half-naked, he hardly would have been content to stay in his room. A chill raced through me at the thought of his hands on me again, and I pushed the memory aside.

We perused the later issues, hoping for more information, but there was not much—these articles were much smaller, barely taking up a corner, and only mentioned that I still had not been found. It reiterated the cash reward on offer for any information. The last one had been published only a month later, and there were no more after that. I tried not to let that get to me, but my jaw clenched—barely four weeks and they'd written me off.

Since there was nothing more to be discovered, we returned the folders to the archives and thanked the clerk for his help. Just as we were about to leave, the door burst open, and a red-haired, freckled-faced young man rushed in.

"Miss Marton?" he asked eagerly, his face bright with excitement. He wore a perfectly pressed suit and tie, and his shoes were so shiny I thought I might blind myself if I looked at them too long. "I'm Hulam Rice, a journalist here. I'd love to interview you if you have a moment." He stuck out a hand.

"Remember, any publicity regarding your return might be help-ful," Fenris said in mindspeak as I hesitated. *"Doing the interview probably won't hurt."*

"All right." I returned the handshake with a smile. "I would be happy to do an interview," I said to the reporter. "So long as it is a brief one. I have a busy day ahead of me."

"I completely understand," he assured me. "This will only take a few minutes."

The reporter pulled out his notepad and pen, and Fenris silently melted into the background as we began. Mr. Rice asked all the questions I expected—why had I run away from home? Where had I gone? How had I managed to maintain myself at such a youthful age? Why had I decided to come back now? How did it feel to return to Haralis after being gone so long? I answered the questions as calmly as I could, but under Fenris's coaching, allowed myself to get a little emotional when telling the reporter about the reasons for my escape. The reporter's sympathetic expression told me I was on the right track—I didn't want to play the victim, but I did want the public on my side. Some would think I was simply a gold digger trying to take advantage of a tragedy, and I needed to forestall such impressions as much as possible.

"What are you going to do once you've claimed your inheritance?" Mr. Rice demanded, scribbling on his notepad. "Are you planning on permanently moving back to Haralis?"

I shrugged. "I can't say yet," I told him. "I've done much traveling these past years, and there are many lovely spots where I might settle. But over the next few days, I will reacquaint myself with Haralis, and perhaps the city and its people will entice me to remain." I gave him a flirtatious smile.

The reporter smiled. "Not to belittle your experience, but it must have been quite freeing, in a way, getting to travel so extensively at an early age."

"It was," I admitted. "To be fair, it wasn't easy to accustom myself to a life of labor after a privileged childhood, but ultimately it may have been good for me. And, of course, life is very different on the Central Continent, and I am happy I got to visit other countries."

"It has been a long time since I've traveled," the journalist said enviously. "I had hoped to be sent to Solantha to cover Chief Mage Iannis ar'Sannin's wedding—it's the talk of the Federation since he is marrying a shifter hybrid. But alas, someone else gets to go."

My eyebrows winged up. "A Chief Mage, marrying a shifter?"

"Not just a shifter," Mr. Rice said. "She's also half-mage *and* his apprentice. I'm honestly surprised you haven't heard about this," he added, looking incredulous.

"Well, as I said, I've been living abroad. I haven't paid too much attention to Federation politics or social gossip."

"Ah, right." The reporter changed the subject. "Are your aunt and uncle aware of your return? They appear in the Haralis society magazines every so often. I'm certain our own social editor will want to reach out to you for an interview as well."

"I haven't spoken to them yet, but I have visited my family lawyer. He will have no doubt informed them. The Finance Secretary is also looking into the matter. I am confident the case will be settled soon," I added with a smile.

The reporter wrapped up the interview, then asked if I would allow a staff photographer to take a picture, which I declined. I didn't want my face appearing in the news, in case it somehow got back to the Watawis Mages Guild, or to someone I'd gone to veterinary school with. Fenris and I bid the reporter goodbye, then headed out to stroll the city a bit more.

"You did well in the interview," Fenris told me as we walked. *"Charming, and very easy to empathize with. Hopefully, it's the way the reporter will paint you when he publishes the interview."*

"That would be preferable," I agreed. It would make it harder for Miss Dorax and my family to deny my claim...but even so, an uneasy feeling roiled in my gut. As we were leaving, the reporter had said he was going to contact my aunt and uncle to get their side of the story. Would his opinion of me change once he spoke to them? What would they even say?

"There's no point in brooding about it," Fenris said, correctly reading my mood. "We may as well enjoy the day. What do you say we get some ice cream?" He pointed to a building across the street.

My eyes widened as I looked where he was pointing. "That's the same parlor my parents took me to as a child!" I exclaimed. Nostalgia filled me as we approached the cheery red and white building. Suddenly I had a hankering for their blueberry-swirl ice cream.

Fenris chuckled. "I'll take that as a yes, then."

We ordered two cones to go, then strolled back to the hotel, discussing our plans in mindspeak along the way. *"You will need to inform your aunt and uncle of your return,"* Fenris said as he licked his mint chocolate chip ice cream. People looked strangely at the old mage with the green ice cream dribbling into his beard, but he seemed oblivious to their reactions. *"It will not do for them to find out through the local newspaper or your lawyer. We only just met with him this morning, so it's likely he hasn't told them yet."*

I nodded. *"I can't say I'm looking forward to it, but it must be done. I'll send them a letter by messenger when we get back to the hotel to announce my return and where I am staying."* That way, I would not have to confront them directly with the shock—they would be somewhat prepared by the time we met.

Or at least as prepared as one can be when someone comes back from the dead.

15

MINA

After sending off a brief, matter-of-fact message to my relatives and enjoying a light lunch at the hotel restaurant, I decided to indulge in a bit of shopping. My two new outfits really weren't enough if I was going to stay in Haralis for any length of time—it would be unseemly for a wealthy woman to be seen in the same suits over and over again, especially when visiting the Mages Guild.

Besides, I wanted to make an impression on my aunt and uncle, and especially my cousin Vanley, when I finally came face-to-face with them. I wanted them to see that I was a grown woman, fully independent and capable of making my own decisions, and that they no longer had any control over me. Wearing well-cut, pretty clothes was empowering in its own way—rather like donning armor. And I planned to arm myself as well as I possibly could for this battle.

Fenris elected to skip out of the shopping spree in favor of visiting some specialty bookshops in the Mages Quarter, which was just as well. We would draw the wrong kind of attention if a much older man who was not my husband or my legal guardian was taking me about town and buying me fancy things. It was a shame Fenris had to continue keeping up that old-mage guise—in his natural form, his ruggedly masculine looks would draw plenty of admiring gazes from the ladies.

As I strolled amongst expensive boutiques I had been too young to shop in when I'd last lived in the city, I wondered what would be best suited to blow Fenris's mind while still being respectable. Was that even possible, considering how worldly he was? That he could look at Miss Dorax with indifference proved he was not easy to impress—her dramatic coloring and air of self-confidence would be very attractive to most men.

And why does that matter? I asked myself. *He's attracted to you, isn't he? Surely he'll like whatever you wear, so long as he gets to peel it off you later.*

My body warmed at the thought of Fenris undressing me, skimming his calloused hands over my bare skin with that careful reverence he always showed. He always acted as if he were unwrapping a long-awaited present, and it made me feel special, cherished.

Some hours later, I emerged from a fashionable shoe shop with a significantly lighter purse. I'd bought three pairs to go with the three dresses I'd just ordered from the tailor a few streets down, all of which would be delivered to the hotel later today. I'd purchased a number of accessories as well. I felt a little guilty about the expense but reminded myself I still had more gold at home. Besides, it had been a long time since I'd allowed myself a splurge. Once I got my fortune back, I would never have to worry about the cost of clothes or accessories again.

"Mina!" a male voice called, and I turned to see a young mage in blue robes hurrying up the street. There were two other mages with him—a pretty brunette girl in leaf green and a tall man in red.

"Maxin?" I asked as recognition dawned on me. I knew these three—they'd been my classmates long ago in the exclusive preparatory school for young mages I had attended. "By the Lady, look how grown up you are!" He'd filled out quite a bit, with broad shoulders and sharper features than the young teen I remembered.

Maxin laughed. "I can say the same about you! You were right, Troina," he said, turning to the brunette. "It's really her."

"How could you doubt me?" Troina brushed past Maxin and enveloped me in a hug. I started in surprise, then hugged her back—I hadn't quite expected such a warm reception. We had been friends, but that had been so long ago I thought she would have forgotten all about me. "I can't believe you're here!" she exclaimed, her dark eyes wide with amazement as she held me out at arm's length to study me. "Everyone said you were dead!"

"So I hear." I smiled wryly.

The three of them pulled me into a nearby coffee shop, where they demanded I spill the beans. Sipping a dark roast, I told them the same story I'd told the reporter—I'd fled that night to escape the abuse and neglect from my relatives, and had spent most of my time abroad until recently.

"I wondered why you'd been holed up in that house so long," Troina said when I finished. "You poor thing—I wish you would have told me, but we were so young. I doubt I would have been able to help." She sighed.

"There's no need to feel guilty," I assured her. "I'm dealing with it now, and that's what matters. How have you been? I've obviously missed out on quite a bit by being gone all these years."

Troina beamed. "This dashing young man and I are to be married next year," she said, placing a hand on Maxin's shoulder. "And our friend Baron here is going to be one of the groomsmen." She pointed to her other companion. He was quiet, with dark hair and spectacles. I suspected that of their trio, he was the more reasonable, practical one.

"What that really means is I will be holding Maxin's hair out of the way while he hurls his guts up at his bachelor party," Baron said dryly, and the others laughed. "In fact, I might be doing that tonight, too."

"Oh?" I raised a brow. "Are you going to a party?"

"Yes, and you should come with us!" Troina's eyes sparkled. "It will be fun—everyone will be so shocked to see you've returned! You'll be the talk of the evening, no doubt about it."

I bit my lip. "I'm not certain I want to be the center of so much attention."

"Oh, don't worry about it." Troina waved a hand. "It's not some big soiree—just a gathering with other mages our age from the city and environs. You won't even need to bring an escort, though you are welcome to."

"It *has* been a long time since I've last been to a party," I admitted. One of the cocktail dresses I'd just purchased, a shimmering mint green, might be just right for the occasion.

"The address is not far from here," Troina pressed. "Really, it's a lot of fun. We all know each other. Many of the people who will be there tonight went to school with us. They will be delighted to see you."

Giving in, I jotted down the address, then went back to the hotel, my mind still whirling from the unexpected encounter. My second day back in Haralis, and I was already going out to a party—with friends, no less! This was certainly not how I'd envisioned things going...and an apprehensive part of me wondered if I would enjoy the party. All the other mages there would be either finishing up or past their apprenticeships by now. Would I be able to fit in? Would I even want to?

If you are to reclaim your identity, it's important for you to be on good terms with the other mages your age, I told myself. And besides, it wasn't as if this were some grand ball. It was just a friendly gathering.

By the time I returned to the hotel, Fenris was already there —sitting by the window in his room, his feet kicked up on the table as he read from an old-looking text. "I see you've acquired some new reading material," I said as I sat in the chair across from him.

Smiling, he removed his boots from the table and put the book aside. "I've brought back several good finds, yes. How did your shopping go?"

"Well enough. I purchased some new outfits, which should arrive soon. And while I was out, I ran into some friends."

"Friends?" Fenris's eyebrows rose. "From your childhood?"

I nodded and told him about my encounter with Troina, Maxin, and Baron, and my decision to go to the party tonight. "Would you like to come?" I asked. "She said I was welcome to bring an escort."

Fenris shook his head. "An old man like me would look out of place at such a gathering," he said. "I'll use the time to find out what Gelisia is up to."

I frowned—in my excitement, I'd nearly forgotten about Miss Dorax. "Do be careful," I said, rising from my chair to kiss him. "I would hate it if you ended up in hot water on my behalf."

"I'll do my best." Fenris slid his arms around me for a proper kiss. I lingered in his embrace for a few moments, simply enjoying the feel of him, then went to my own room to shower and hopefully dress if my purchases arrived once I was finished. I had a party to get ready for, after all, and I was woefully out of practice with cosmetics.

16

FENRIS

After Mina went off to her own room to primp for the party, I did a bit of tinkering with my own appearance. Slipping into the privacy of my bathroom, I cast an illusion spell. When I eventually emerged from the back entrance of the hotel, I wore the guise of a weedy, nondescript human male dressed casually in jeans and a gray t-shirt.

The palace was only a few blocks away, so I chose to walk, tucking my hands into my pockets. I was once again reminded of Solantha as I strolled about the beautiful city—the briny breeze blowing in off the coast and the artsy sections of town woven in between classic architecture were all reminiscent of Canalo's capital city.

Even so, Haralis didn't fill me with the same sense of home that Solantha did. The city felt more like a coastal vacation spot and less like a cultural hub, and though Haralis Palace was impressive with its sparkling stone exterior and towering turrets, it didn't hold a candle to Solantha Palace. There were no close friends here, like Iannis and Sunaya, no motherly cook and helpful librarian, no pesky ether parrot...

Better to stop comparing, I told myself as a pang of homesickness hit me in the stomach. *You're never going back there, so there is no point in torturing yourself with memories.*

I found a coffee shop just across the street from the palace and ordered coffee and a pastry, which I enjoyed at a window seat right by the door. From my vantage point, I could easily watch the entrance of the palace and see who was coming and going.

I sat there for nearly an hour and had refilled my coffee twice before anything interesting happened—plenty of people came and went, but they were unimportant, no one I recognized. But just as I was getting sick of the brew, a dark, official-looking steamcar came around from the palace's garage entrance, and I spotted Gelisia sitting in the backseat.

Just who I was looking for.

I hurriedly slapped a coin on the tablecloth, then rushed out to the line of steamcabs waiting at the corner and flagged one down. I regretted my decision almost immediately—a mere block away, we hit a snarl of traffic so dense I would have been better off following on foot. It seemed like all of Haralis was returning home from work at the same time.

A bicycle would be very handy right now, I thought, but there was nothing for it. Sunaya would simply hop on her steambike to tail her suspect, but I was not comfortable riding them. Besides, hardly anyone seemed to use them around here. A steambike would stick out like a sore thumb.

A good twenty minutes later, Gelisia's car finally turned off the main roads and into a wealthy residential neighborhood. I ordered the cab driver to turn down the same street, and we followed Gelisia at a discreet distance. Her driver pulled up to the curb in front of a large mansion, and I watched from a block away as Gelisia sashayed up the steps and rang the doorbell, leaving the car at the curb to wait for her.

I paid for the ride, then got out of my cab and raced around the block to a quiet side street at the other side of the mansion. A quick flex of my legs, and I bounded over the six-foot iron fence with ease, landing with barely a whisper in the garden. A shed stood a few feet away from me, and I quickly grabbed a gardener's hat and a rake. No one but the gardener himself would suspect I was trespassing.

With the rake in hand, I casually strolled to the front of the mansion and busied myself raking nonexistent leaves from the pristine lawn. Though evening was approaching, the days were long enough now that there was still sufficient light by which to garden.

To my amusement, Gelisia was still standing by the door, tapping her foot in impatience. She paid me no notice as the front door opened.

"Good afternoon, ma'am," a servant in a neatly pressed maid's uniform said. "May I help you?"

"Finance Secretary Dorax to see Mr. and Mrs. Cantorin," Gelisia said, handing the maid a card from a small, silver-engraved box. "It's an urgent matter."

The servant invited Gelisia in, and I discreetly moved over to the planter right beneath the front window where the parlor was. To my delight, the window had been propped open, and I could hear perfectly as Gelisia sat down on one of the chairs and the servant promised to bring her tea. Bending my head, I pretended to weed the riotous patches of blossoms while keeping my ears pricked for any sign of conversation.

It wasn't long before I heard footsteps. "Miss Dorax," a male voice said. "To what do we owe this visit?"

"I am here regarding your missing niece, Tamina Marton," Gelisia said. "A young woman has turned up, claiming to be her, and eager to wrest her inheritance back from your family."

"Can it really be little Tamina?" a female voice—Mrs. Cantorin, I assumed—asked in wonder. There was a rustle of skirts and a creak of wood that told me she and her husband had sat down as well. Pulling myself up the closest tree trunk, I risked a quick peek—sure enough, a middle-aged couple was sitting on a small couch across from Gelisia. The man had dark blond hair, a waspish face, and looked to be reed-thin beneath his robes, whereas his wife was plumper, with honey-brown hair and softer, more open features. None of them were looking in my direction, and I quickly turned my attention to the branches, pretending to prune them.

"That is startling news indeed. We had long given up hope of Tamina being alive," Mr. Cantorin said briskly. There was a distinct tone of annoyance in his voice, and I felt a flash of anger —to him, Mina was little more than a nuisance. "She had been moody and strange the last few weeks before her disappearance, making up the most awful stories about our son. But even so, her drowning like that was a terrible shock, particularly to my wife. I would hate for that old wound to be reopened by some grasping gold digger."

"Your son is Vanley Cantorin, correct?" Gelisia had a notepad and a pen in her hand. "Is he in residence?"

I glanced over to see Mrs. Cantorin shift uneasily in her seat. "He has already left for some party, as usual," she said, and there was the slightest note of censure in her voice. "He will not be back until much later."

"That is quite all right," Gelisia said. "I really only need to interview the two of you. You are Tamina's closest surviving relative and universal heir, Mrs. Cantorin. Tell me more about your niece, so I can determine if this girl is indeed her."

I hope Vanley is not attending the same party Mina is at, I thought as I busied myself with the branches again. I felt a quick tug of concern, and briefly wondered if I should go to the party in disguise so I could watch over her before I remembered the protection spell I'd put on her.

Mina will be fine, I told myself firmly. Finding out what Gelisia was up to was more important. Besides, Mina could handle herself. She would be with her friends, and she had her magic.

"Mina was a difficult and reserved child, but we tried to make allowances for her bereavement, and I was sincerely grieved at her disappearing like that," Mrs. Cantorin said, as if she were trying to soothe the harshness of her husband's words. Her tone rang with sincerity, and I wondered if perhaps she was unaware of what had truly happened to Mina. "If she is indeed alive, we will thank the Creator. If you like, I can give you some photos taken when she stayed here and handwriting samples from her schoolwork. They should be somewhere in the attic."

"That is hardly necessary, Mrs. Cantorin," Gelisia demurred. "I would not get your hopes up. I am almost certain that the girl is an imposter. Indeed, I suspect she is merely the puppet of the sinister old mage who travels with her and that this man is coaching her on what to say. Who knows, he may be an international criminal who seeks out large fortunes and systematically swindles the true heirs."

Despite the outrageousness of her statement, I had to grin at this flattering description. Being dishonest herself, naturally Gelisia would be quick to ascribe nefarious motives to anyone else.

"I see," Mr. Cantorin said in a clipped voice. "Perhaps we should have expected such an attempt to be made, given the size of Miss Marton's fortune, but we could not possibly have imagined such a despicable level of subterfuge."

"Using the tragic fate of our dead niece against us," Mrs. Cantorin said in a soft, scandalized whisper. "It's unconscionable!"

"I completely agree," Gelisia said with false sympathy. I gritted my teeth. She was supposed to be an impartial investigator, yet it appeared she'd already made up her mind and was trying to sway the investigation!

Once a manipulator, always a manipulator.

"I strongly advise you not to meet this girl before the hearing next week," Gelisia continued. "She and her escort may spout any number of lies to draw you to their side, and older mages like this Mr. ar'Tarnis can be particularly crafty. I would not be surprised if he had some coercion spell at the ready and is only waiting until he can get you alone."

"We will order the staff not to admit them if they come calling," Mr. Cantorin promised as I bristled. Coercion indeed! The only person who was using coercion around here was Gelisia herself. But there was nothing I could do about that right now. We had been planning on paying a visit to the Cantorin family, but it sounded like that would not be possible now.

"An excellent precaution," Gelisia said smoothly. "Mind you, there is a slight possibility I am wrong and the girl truly is the missing heiress. If her claim is substantiated, I shall order an audit of the accounts to ensure that no monies went missing from her fortune during your stewardship. The past thirteen years' expenses and taxes will be checked with a fine-tooth comb."

There was a long silence, and I could practically see Gelisia's cat-like smile, though I was still busying myself with the landscaping. While a part of me was still seething at her greedy, manipulative tactics, I had to admire the deft way in which she wielded them. I could hardly blame the Cantorin family, or even the Chief Mage of Innarta, for being taken in—even I had been fooled.

"I'm sure that won't be necessary," Mr. Cantorin finally said. "As you said, the girl is likely an imposter, manipulated and coached by that old mage she is with." Another pause and then, "While you are here, Secretary, is there by chance any particular charity you support to which we may make a sizeable contribution? We have not quite yet met our quota of charitable deductions for the year."

"What a generous offer," Gelisia purred, and I could just imagine the seductive gleam in her eye. "As a matter of fact, I recently set up a charity called the Dorax Fund, which aims to support indigent students in Faricia. We are just getting started and would greatly appreciate any support you can give."

I lifted my head again to watch as the Cantorins handed over a hundred gold coins, with a promise of five hundred more once the "commotion" was all over.

"Your generosity is greatly appreciated," Gelisia assured them. "This will all blow over very soon, and you will be able to go back to your lives as if this never happened."

The Cantorins bid Gelisia goodbye, and I bent my head over the planter again as the front door opened. Gelisia didn't even look around, and I watched from my perch in the tree as she sauntered down the path with an insufferably smug look on her beautiful face. I wondered what she would think if she knew that her former boss, Polar ar'Tollis, was watching her now in the guise of a gardener, planning to foil her machinations.

That fantasy will never come to fruition, I thought with bitter regret as she got back into the car, nodding to the driver to set off. I would never be able to confront Gelisia as myself, to rub into her face that not only was I alive, but thriving. The knowledge that she had not achieved the coveted position of Chief Mage would have to be enough. Preventing her dastardly scheme against Mina would be my own form of retribution.

"Do you really think this is wise?" Mrs. Cantorin asked, and I pushed all thoughts of Gelisia out of my mind to focus on their conversation. The couple was still in the parlor, within easy hearing. "What if this girl really is our niece? We cannot simply deny her what is rightfully hers."

"We had better hope she isn't," Mr. Cantorin snapped. "If Tamina really is back from the dead, she will ruin us. We have been spending her money this entire time and will never be able to refill her coffers."

"Have we really spent that much of it?" Mrs. Cantorin asked, her voice faint with shock. "I know we've dipped into her funds a time or two, but..."

"A time or two?" Mr. Cantorin laughed harshly. "My dear, our income would never cover all the parties and cruises, the hunting trips and golf outings, all the new outfits you buy—our life of luxury is entirely thanks to Tamina's fortune. If she were to return, we would be disgraced. Society will shun us forever."

Shaking my head in disgust, I turned away and headed around the side of the mansion. I'd heard more than enough.

I hope the Cantorins have not spent too *much of Mina's fortune,* I thought grimly as I headed back to the hotel. Getting justice was one thing, but Mina deserved to live in comfort after all the hardship she'd been through, and it would be devastating to learn that the fortune we were working so hard to reclaim had already been squandered.

17

MINA

The party was already in full swing when I arrived at the grand-looking townhouse in the middle of the city's Mages Quarter. Music and light were pouring out of open windows, and the smell of roasted meat and sugary pastries reminded me that I'd skipped dinner. Thanking the cab driver, I pressed a coin into his hand and entered the house with my stomach full of nerves.

At least you look great, I told myself as I handed my coat to the servant just inside the door. The shimmery green cocktail dress fit me like a glove, accentuating my curves, and the matching heels made my calves look fantastic. I'd piled my hair atop my head in loose curls held together with sparkling pins, leaving a few to tumble down the back of my neck and frame the sides of my face. A quick glance in the foyer mirror told me that my makeup was still intact—smoky eyes, jewel-red lips, and the slightest dusting of blush on my cheekbones.

I wish Fenris were here to see me.

I'd gone back to Fenris's room to show him my outfit before I'd left, but he'd disappeared. He'd left a note on the table letting me know that he'd gone out on an "errand"—for Fenris, that could mean anything from visiting a business connection to perusing the shelves in a dusty bookshop full of old manuscripts. I smiled a little at that—it must be freeing for him to be able to rummage through magical bookshops again, even if he did have to go in the guise of an old man. He was right not to come along to the party—he would have looked completely out of place.

And besides, I reminded myself, *there's no reason you can't show him the dress when you return to the hotel tonight.*

The thought filled me with a rush of warmth that banished my nerves, and just in time, too. "Mina!" Troina exclaimed as she moved through the crowd toward me. She wore a brilliant red dress with a glittering pattern on the side that formed a rose and drew the eye to her curvy hips. "You made it! And just look at that dress," she gushed, looking me up and down. "You'll be the talk of the party tonight."

Indeed, I observed as she hooked her arm through mine, I was getting quite a few looks. Curiosity and interest from the men, and a few jealous looks from the women. Suddenly, I felt self-conscious about showing so much skin. I'd never worn such a revealing dress in my life—there had been no occasion to do so growing up, and in veterinary school and Abbsville there were no parties that required something as fancy as a cocktail dress.

I could just imagine the faces of the book club ladies if they saw me in this. A few of the older ones would keel over in shock at the sight.

Doing my best to ignore the stares, I allowed Troina to drag me over to her group of friends, who were gathered around the couches in a salon just off to the side of the entrance. This was a party, rather than a formal ball, and there wasn't a single mage here in robes, or much over thirty years old. Troina's fiancé and their friend Baron greeted me enthusiastically, and I was introduced to ten other people whose names flitted out of my head as quickly as they'd gone in.

"Is it true, then, that you've been living amongst humans for the past ten years?" a brunette with dramatic blue eye shadow exclaimed after I'd been handed a drink. "My, how terrible that must have been! However could you bear it?"

"It was hard, at first," I said, doing my best to suppress the instinctive protest that came to my lips at her obvious horror. "But I wouldn't say it was *terrible* by any means. Humans aren't barbarians."

"Of course not," the man sitting next to her said smoothly. "Brialtha only meant that having to survive on your own, without any magic, would be very trying."

"Mina has always been strong-willed and intelligent," Troina declared from her seat next to me. Smiling, she put an arm around my shoulder and hugged me. "I should have known better than to think you'd really died. I'm so happy you're here."

Pleasure filled me at Troina's sincerity. "I'm very glad to be back," I agreed, relaxing a little. While these young mages were strangers, they were not yet hardened to the point of coldness and rigidity, like most older mages eventually became. I felt much more at ease around them than I had at Haralis Palace.

"There are rumors going around that you might not really be Tamina Marton," a tall blonde said, the barest hint of a sneer in her voice.

"That's ridiculous," Troina snapped. "I went to school with Mina and have known her nearly all her life—anybody who knew her would recognize her in an instant."

"Yes," the blonde said silkily, "but it is possible to use magic to change one's appearance in a permanent fashion."

"Those spells are illegal," Maxin, Troina's fiancé, pointed out. "At least in the Federation." While mages embellished and changed their appearance at will, permanently impersonating another mage was forbidden. It made fraud all too easy.

The blonde shrugged. "If I saw a chance at gaining the Marton fortune, I might not hesitate to bend a rule or two."

I opened my mouth to retort, but the blonde turned and disappeared into the crowd. "Don't listen to her," Troina said, squeezing my hand. "Darina has always been a jealous twat. She's just upset because she's no longer the prettiest blonde at the party."

That startled a laugh out of me. "I thought *you* were the prettiest blonde at the party," I teased.

"Yes, and what a shame it is that both of you are sitting on the couch like wallflowers," Maxin said, taking Troina's hand. He tugged her into the next room, which had been fashioned into a dance floor. Before I knew it, another man was asking me to dance. Restless energy from that near confrontation still buzzed in my veins, and I accepted, eager to burn some of it off.

I danced for a good hour and a half, changing partners frequently so as not to favor any man in particular. There was no point in getting anyone's hopes up when I fully intended to warm Fenris's bed tonight. Several asked me questions about my past and my future intentions, but I answered evasively or pretended not to hear them.

As yet another song drew to a close, already melding into the next, I stepped back from my dance partner, intending to go to the refreshments table and rest for a bit. But before I could turn, another man's large hands clamped hard around my waist. The next thing I knew, I was being spun around into another dance.

"Enjoying yourself?" my new "partner" sneered.

When my appalled gaze met his, my heart stopped. Staring down at me, a decade older yet hardly changed, was my cousin Vanley. He'd filled out some since I'd last seen him as a teenager —broader shoulders and chest, thicker arms, and chiseled features that made him deceptively handsome. His thick chestnut-brown hair was styled with some kind of gel that slicked it straight back from his face. His dark eyes were narrowed on mine, his lips curled mockingly, and his large fingers dug tightly into my flesh as he spun me across the dance floor.

"Let go of me," I growled as a wave of revulsion swept through me. To be touched by him yet again, against my will—it was like an old nightmare recurring when I'd least expected it. Anxiety tried to take over, and I felt my skin growing clammy as my stomach pitched, but I pushed it back with a wave of anger instead. "I'm not your property, Vanley."

"I heard a rumor that you were back, but I didn't think it was possible." There was a hint of a slur in his voice, and as we came into the light, I saw that his gaze was blurred. Drinking? Drugs? I had seen a few people passing around pills in the corner. It would be just like Vanley to indulge in such a vice. "You died in the water."

"Is that how this works?" I asked incredulously. "You tell yourself a lie so often that you start to believe it's real? We both know what really happened that night." I wrenched myself out of his grasp. "If you don't leave me alone, I'd be more than happy to do it again."

Vanley sneered. "That was a stroke of luck," he said, taking a step toward me. Heads were turning now, and I realized we were drawing an audience. "I'm a fully trained mage now, and you're a nobody. They won't believe you any more than they did the last time. You should keep your head down if you know what's good for you."

A voice in my head was screaming at me to run, and that only made me angrier. How was it that, over a decade later, Vanley was still trying to bully me around? I raised my hands, fully intending on blasting him with raw magic, no matter the consequences. But before I could summon my power, the air in front of me flared red and Vanley was thrown straight into a group of dancers behind us.

I gaped as they all went down like a bunch of bowling pins, Vanley howling in outrage. What in Recca had happened? Questioning gazes turned my way. I schooled my expression into haughty superiority and turned on my heel. *Let them think I had done that on purpose,* I thought as I strode away. Maybe others would think twice before messing with me.

"Mina!" Maxin grabbed my arm as I walked right by him without seeing him; Troina was standing right next to me, wide-eyed. "Are you all right? What happened?"

"My cousin Vanley was up to his old tricks," I said lightly, shrugging off his grip. "I think I'd like to go home now."

Troina nodded, an understanding expression on her face. "I'll help you catch a cab," she said.

"I'm so sorry this happened to you," Troina murmured as she walked me to the curb. "I'd forgotten Vanley is a regular at these parties."

"It's not your fault." There had to be at least a hundred people in there—Troina couldn't be expected to remember everyone. "I'm glad you invited me, actually," I said, turning to her with a smile. "For the most part, I had a good time."

We embraced with the promise to catch up for coffee again, then parted ways—Troina went back to the party, while I got into the cab that pulled up. As it drove me back to the hotel, I stared out the window, collecting my thoughts and allowing myself to decompress from the evening's excitement. Anxiety and disgust were still churning in my stomach, but as I relaxed, these feelings faded away, replaced by confusion and a certain amount of pride.

I didn't know what happened back there with Vanley, though I suspected that if I asked Fenris, he would have an answer for me. But even if I hadn't blasted Vanley myself, I was proud I'd faced him head-on, that I hadn't turned tail and run away, or allowed him to bully me as I'd done in the past.

And you managed to act like a normal person at the party. I'd mostly fit in, talking and laughing with other mages my own age, even dancing! It had been a long time since I'd done anything more than the simple country dances that the Abbsville residents preferred, but after a few tries, my feet seemed to fall back into the familiar steps.

By the time my steamcar pulled up to the Black Horse, I was practically beaming.

"Fenris!" I exclaimed as I rushed into his room, then stopped short. He was sitting at his breakfast table in his normal guise, a brooding expression on his face as he looked out the window. "Is everything all right?"

"Mina!" His eyes widened with delight as he rose, the dark expression clearing from his handsome face. "You look stunning," he said, his yellow eyes darkening with hunger as they roved up and down me. A flush of heat rose in my chest, and I could feel my cheeks turning pink beneath his regard. But while I had felt exposed when hungry male eyes devoured me at the party, I didn't feel uncomfortable as his gaze trailed across my exposed skin. Instead, I felt...exhilarated.

But I remembered how morose he'd looked when I walked in, and that gave me pause. "I was about to tell you all about the party, but you look like something's troubling you," I said, placing my hands on his broad shoulders. "Did something happen?"

"Nothing that can't wait until later," Fenris murmured, curling his fingers around my waist. He drew me close and kissed me, and I quickly forgot all about Vanley and my concern for Fenris. Wrapping my arms around his neck, I kissed him back, allowing him to pick me up and carry me to the bed, where we made slow, tender love.

"Now that we've gotten that out of our system," I teased much later, scraping the tips of my fingers through the crisp hairs on his chest, "why don't you tell me what's bothering you?"

Fenris sighed, rolling onto his back. He tucked me into his side, wrapping his arm around my shoulder, and said, "I decided to do a bit of reconnaissance while you were at the party."

"Oh?" My stomach tightened at the tone in his voice. "On whom?" I asked, though I had the feeling I already knew.

"Gelisia Dorax. I followed her from the Mages Guild to your aunt and uncle's house."

"She must have been there to interview them about me," I said, tracing lines across Fenris's abdomen. "What questions did she ask them?"

"It was hardly an interview," Fenris scoffed. "More of a shakedown." He proceeded to tell me all about Gelisia's bias, how she was already convinced I was an imposter, and how she'd extorted a bribe from my relatives in exchange for making sure I was "taken care of."

By the time he was finished, I was burning with outrage. "She can't simply *lie* to the Chief Mage," I cried, sitting up in the bed. "That's ridiculous!"

"No doubt she will spin some clever story," Fenris said grimly. "It will be our job to provide compelling evidence to the contrary and reveal her corruption."

"But how are we going to do that?" I raked my hands through my hair, feeling a headache coming on. "No one is going to believe your word—you're a stranger. You certainly can't tell them about your past dealings with her."

"Very true," Fenris said, "but I've been thinking on the matter, and I have some ideas. She is careless because she has gotten away with much in the past, I believe, but that impunity will end soon. In the meantime, we must be extra-vigilant, and you should not go anywhere alone. Gelisia might try to trap you somehow, and someone might even be sent to attack you."

"Attack me!" I exclaimed, alarmed at the possibility. "You mean to say I might be assassinated?"

"People have been killed for much smaller fortunes than yours," Fenris pointed out. "It would be imprudent not to consider the possibility."

"Is that why you put a protection spell on me earlier?" I asked, crossing my arms.

Fenris stilled. "How do you know about it? Did someone try to hurt you?"

"I had a run-in with my cousin Vanley at the party." I told him what happened, then added, "I'm grateful for the spell, but it would have been nice to know about it beforehand."

Fenris winced. "To be honest, I cast it while you were asleep, then forgot about it the next day. I'm very glad you had it, even if you are perfectly capable of taking care of yourself," he added, smoothing a hand over my hair. "I'm proud of you for standing up to that bully."

His touch relaxed me, and some of my headache went away. "I actually feel less stressed about meeting my relatives now that I've faced down Vanley," I confessed as I snuggled back into the sheets with Fenris. "He was the bogeyman I feared for so long, and now that I've vanquished him, I see he really wasn't that much of a threat at all."

"The worst monsters are never the ones who look like them," Fenris murmured. "They're the ones with the pretty faces and the gilded tongues, and they're very good at convincing you they're one of the good ones until they stab you in the back. Remember that."

He kissed my hair, then turned off the light. And as we drifted off to sleep, I couldn't help but wonder what monsters Fenris had encountered in his own past.

18

MINA

I woke to the sun's rays peeking in through the window slats, feeling surprisingly cheerful for someone who had stayed up late and was now getting up at the crack of dawn. The sight of Fenris still tangled in the bed sheets with me, and the warm, fuzzy feeling that had settled in my chest during the night, were enough to make any woman feel content.

Humming, I slipped from the bed and returned to my own room to shower and dress for the day. There was much to be thankful for, I reflected as I stood under the hot spray and lathered up my hair. I had made it back to Haralis, I was alive, and my worst nightmare, Vanley, was nothing but a pathetic user, easily pushed away. He had no power over me anymore, and even if I walked away from this whole ordeal with not a copper in my pocket, the journey would have been worth it for that reason alone.

Since Fenris was still sound asleep, and it was a long time until we were to meet for breakfast at eight, I dressed in casual clothes and went for a walk to reacquaint myself with the city. Strolling through the mages section, I enjoyed the warm sun on my face as it finished its climb over the horizon, taking in the scents of blossoming flowers from neighborhood gardens and listening to the twitter of birds as they flitted from tree to tree across the boulevard.

Nostalgia swept through me as I passed through Northgate Park, where my mother had taken me as a child to fly kites. At this time of day, it was completely empty aside from a few mages and servants walking their dogs. I was tempted to climb on the playground equipment just to see if it would feel the same as it had when I was young, but I refrained.

Across the street was the depot for the streetcar that traveled daily from the Mages Quarter to the city zoo—another series of fond memories, this time with my grandmother. She had loved taking me to see the exotic animals. With something of a talent for drawing, she had always taken out her leather-bound sketchbook to draw the monkeys and the lions. A pang went through me as I wondered if those sketchbooks still lay somewhere in my grandmother's house, or if they'd been lost.

She would have stored them in a trunk somewhere. Drawing may not have been my grandmother's purpose in life, but she had loved it enough that she would not have simply thrown the sketchbooks away.

As the hour drew closer to six, people started emerging onto the streets, some hurrying to work, others strolling to the nearest café to grab a cup of coffee and the morning paper. Enticed by the smell of fresh roast, I ducked into a café and ordered coffee and a pastry, then sat down at a small table so I could peruse the paper. Perhaps the reporter I'd spoken with the other day, Mr. Rice, had published our interview. I wasn't certain if I was nervous or excited about the prospect, but I knew I had to see it for myself.

Sure enough, there was a full-page article with the headline "Missing Heiress Returns" on page two that I carefully scanned. While the journalist had faithfully recounted our interview, he'd also, as promised, included a quote from my Uncle Bobb. In it, Bobb stated that the Cantorin family was outraged that some avaricious imposter could just waltz into town and try to claim their long-dead niece's inheritance. Only someone cruel and unfeeling would dare to attempt such a scheme and stir up the family's barely-healed grief.

I rolled my eyes at that. The only grief my relatives were experiencing was the possibility that they might soon lose the fortune they'd been squandering. *My fortune.* Fenris's eavesdropping last night had confirmed that my uncle had not deigned to wait the statutory period before dipping his fingers into my coffers, and I had no doubt they'd spent a sizable portion of it. A lot could happen over thirteen years.

Speaking of fortunes...the bottom portion of the article contained a rough estimate of the inheritance I stood to gain— or rather, as the piece said, the Cantorin family stood to lose. My eyes widened as I read the sum several times—I had no idea my grandmother's fortune had been that large! I had known she was rich, but, according to the journalist, it was one of the largest fortunes in the state.

I wonder what Fenris will say when I read this to him over breakfast, I thought. Suddenly, I remembered his warning to me last night about not going anywhere by myself. My cheeks flushed guiltily, and I ducked my head behind the paper, as if Fenris might walk by any moment, looking for me.

I'd better hurry back to the hotel. Quickly, I finished off my pastry, then paid my tab and rushed back down the street. It took me only half a block to remember that it was a good thirty-minute walk back to the hotel, and I forced myself to slow down. There was no point in winding myself trying to get back, especially since there were so many people out and about. It wasn't as if I were traipsing down dark alleys. No one was going to try to attack me in broad daylight, not in this rich part of town.

Determined not to let some unseen threat get the better of me, I smiled and began to hum a tune under my breath as I walked. The mages, who thought I was a human, ignored me, but the other humans passing on the street smiled and nodded greetings. As I smiled back, I wondered what they would think if they knew I was not one of their own.

Are you really so different? I asked myself. Yes, I had magic, but I'd spent almost half my life living as a human. Though the residents of Abbsville had simpler problems to cope with than mages in their grand residences and lofty halls, in the end, they weren't that different. We all *looked* the same—the only difference was in how we got things done.

And the fact you'll outlive them by five times their normal lifespan.

That was the main reason I'd never taken a human beau in Abbsville—I'd worried I might fall in love with someone, and then where would I be? Humans and mages had married before, obviously—the first mages had sprung from humans. But it would be too much for me to bear, to live my first hundred years by the side of a husband who would age far too quickly and would die while I looked to still be in my first blush of youth.

Fenris, at least, would live to be a few hundred years old. Perhaps even older. He was not an ordinary shifter, and there was something ageless about his demeanor. If he one day came out and told me he was immortal, I wasn't sure I'd be surprised.

Okay, well, maybe a revelation like that *would* surprise me. But not nearly as much as it would coming from anyone else.

I was crossing a side street, only a block from the hotel, when a large black steamcar that had been parked on the curb suddenly came to life with a huge belch of steam, accelerating for all it was worth. My heart leapt into my throat as I realized it was headed straight for me, and I dove out of the way. The car barreled past me with barely an inch to spare, then wheeled around with a dexterity that was surprising for its size, only to hurtle straight for me again.

By the Lady, I thought as my life flashed before my eyes. *I'm going to die.*

Adrenaline slammed into me, and I did the only thing I could think of. Seconds before the car crashed into me, I jumped onto the hood. It was a stupid move—the car's chassis was high enough that my feet only landed on the bumper instead of the hood itself—but just as I was about to be crushed against the building behind me, an unseen force pushed me up, past the windshield, and onto the top of the car. Unfortunately, I was unable to keep up with the momentum—I tripped and fell off the car's back, landing hard on my shoulder as the vehicle plowed into the brick wall. A high-pitched shriek from the steam engine nearly blew out my eardrums. When I clapped my hands to my ears, my shoulder barked in pain.

Move. You need to move!

Heart pounding, I scrambled to my feet, ignoring my pain and confusion as best I could. As I straightened, I caught sight of the driver through the window—a white, middle-aged male, his face bleeding from broken window glass. The hand rubbing his eyes was only making the blood smeared across his face messier. I nearly felt a moment's pity for him before I remembered he had just tried to murder me.

I looked around for witnesses or enforcers, but despite the noise, the street was still empty. Only a mangy, thin cat had seen the attack on me from a first-floor windowsill. A throb of pain reminded me I was hurt, and I looked down at my shoulder. My shirt was torn, and through it, I had a nasty case of road rash. An attempt to roll my shoulder joint had me gritting my teeth to keep from screaming—I had dislocated it in the fall. And though I'd popped dislocated joints back in before, on both animals and on humans, I felt positively squeamish about doing it to myself.

Steeling myself, I turned back to the steamcar, but it was already moving away, rolling sluggishly toward the opposite corner. I thought about giving pursuit, but I was in no shape to do so with my injuries. My heart sank as I watched it retreat—by the time I told anyone about this, the car would have already disappeared into the avenue's busy morning traffic.

Moving as fast as I could without jarring my shoulder further, I went around the back of the hotel and climbed the stairs to my room. If the hotel staff saw me like this, they would have questions that I was not ready to answer. My mind was still buzzing with adrenaline and shock—I could barely string together two sentences in my head.

A sob of relief tore from my throat as I finally reached my door. I got it open, then hurried into the adjoining room. "Fenris," I croaked as he sat up, his face still heavy with sleep.

"Mina!" Fenris's eyes widened in alarm, and he jumped out of the bed, fully naked. The sight momentarily distracted me from my pain, but then he was by my side, and I hissed in pain as he gently took me by the arms. "What happened?"

"My shoulder," I groaned, and he let go immediately.

"I see," he said gravely, his yellow gaze going to my torn shirt. Carefully, he guided me onto the bed, then pursed his lips as he studied the area.

"This isn't something I'm going to be able to heal with magic, not right away," he warned. "I'm going to have to set your shoulder manually."

I nodded—it was the same with broken bones. If I tried to heal them before setting them, they would knit back together incorrectly, and I would have to break them again or leave the patient permanently disfigured.

"Just do it quickly," I said through my teeth.

Fenris helped me lie flat on the bed, with my injured arm facing outward. I squeezed my eyes shut as he took my wrist in his hand and slowly began to pull my arm away from my body in a ninety-degree angle. I sucked in a sharp breath as pain stabbed through me, but a few seconds later, I felt a *clunk*, and the pain immediately plummeted to a more manageable level.

"Phew." I let out the breath I'd been holding. "Thank you."

"You're welcome," Fenris said tightly. He pressed a hand against my shoulder, and cool, sweet relief flooded me as he used his magic to heal the tender joint and the shredded skin. After a few moments, he sat back, and my stomach dropped at the look on his face. His jaw was set, and his eyes gleamed with anger.

"Would you like to explain to me," he said softly, "what you were doing outside by yourself?"

I swallowed hard, pushing myself into an upright position— I didn't like lying prone beneath his gaze while he was looking at me like that. "I...you were asleep, and I didn't think I'd be out long," I said lamely. "I just wanted to go for a walk and enjoy the sunrise." I gave him my best puppy-dog face.

Fenris scrubbed a hand over his face. "Mina, you look like you've just been run over by a car," he said in a pained voice. "Didn't we just have a discussion last night about you not going out by yourself?"

"I'm sorry," I groaned, pressing my palms against my eyes. "I only remembered after I was already out, and I hurried back as fast as I could. I'm not used to all this. I've never had anyone try to kill me before."

"I know." Fenris's tone softened, and he put his arm around my shoulder. "Sometimes, I forget that you have not been exposed to the same dangers I have," he said gently, rubbing my back.

I swallowed against the lump in my throat. "I've never

thought of myself as naïve, but after today…" I raised my head to look at him, and my heart settled a little at the compassion in his gaze. "I know you said that someone might try to kill me, but I didn't believe it, not really, until that steamcar tried to mow me down."

"So it was a car, then?" Fenris's jaw clenched. "What happened, exactly?"

I told him about how the vehicle had come out of nowhere only a block from the hotel, in the only deserted spot anywhere close by, and had nearly run me down twice before I'd managed to get away. "I think your protection charm saved me again," I said. "It gave me a boost and helped me jump over the car before it could crush me into the wall."

Fenris shook his head. "I am doubly glad I decided to put that spell on you, but it may not save you next time," he warned. "You must promise me that you will not leave my side again, Mina. When this is over, you may go wherever you choose, but until then, I want you within my line of sight at all times."

I nodded, snuggling in a little tighter against him. "I'm happy to stay by your side," I said, resting my cheek against his chest. The warm, steady heartbeat thumping just beneath his skin reassured me, and my cheeks warmed as I suddenly remembered that he was naked.

Fenris nuzzled the top of my head, then gently extricated himself from my grip. "As much as I would love to spend a bit more time with you in my arms, you are still tender, and I should shower and dress for the day," he said ruefully. "We cannot remain here, waiting for the next attack. I'll make arrangements to protect you better."

I sighed as he retreated toward the bathroom, watching his muscled backside. Of all the ways my morning could have gone, why hadn't I just stayed in bed so I could start with *that*?

19

FENRIS

After that narrow escape, Mina and I decided to relocate to a beach hotel just a few minutes outside the city, where it would be harder for our enemies to track us. We asked the Black Horse to forward any mail in case we heard from the Mages Guild or Mr. Ransome but not to give out our new address to anyone whatsoever.

As we sat in the sand, sipping drinks from cups garnished with umbrellas, we did our best to enjoy the sun and the salty breeze and not to think too much about the near-fatal accident or the upcoming hearing. Mina certainly deserved a period of relaxation after the shock and stress she had suffered.

The first thing Mina had asked back at the Black Horse, once she'd calmed down from her run-in with the steamcar, was who might have ordered the hit. The obvious suspects were Mina's aunt and uncle. While I did not put such a crime past Gelisia, she had no motive that I could see.

"Do you think it could have been Vanley?" Mina had wondered, twirling a lock of her hair nervously. "As retribution for knocking him on his ass at the party?"

I'd shrugged. "Men have killed women for less," I said, "but you mentioned he was inebriated and perhaps even drugged, so who knows if he even remembers the incident very well."

Mina nodded. "He was acting as if he wasn't sure if I was a hallucination," she admitted. "He might very well have convinced himself the next day that nothing had happened at all." Her lips curved into a grim smile. "He's going to be in for a real shock at the hearing."

The hearing. We needed to devise a strategy to counter the probable outcome—I could already see Gelisia sauntering up to the Chief Mage and declaring that Mina was an imposter, that she had no right to the Marton Estate. We would present our own side of the story, and I was confident we would ultimately prevail. Yet, unless we firmly established Mina's identity among the people of Haralis, questions would always remain.

This posed a dilemma. For her safety, I would have liked to tuck Mina away where nobody else had access to her, but in the long run, and even to make a credible showing in the impending hearing, she needed to stay as visible in the mage community as possible. The more people who saw and recognized her, who believed she had returned, the better.

The desire to hide her from everyone else partly sprang from pure selfishness; I wanted to keep her at my side, and my wolfish side growled at the very idea of Mina looking at another mage, of her being courted by anyone else. But I had to put her welfare first. Once she had regained her rights, I would encourage her to accept the invitations that even now drifted in from various mage families. No matter what I might wish and hope for, I had no illusions that we were going to end up as lifetime mates. Mina's predicament was nearly at an end—she would be free to step back into the limelight, and she deserved a man who could stand proudly, openly, at her side.

Not one who had to skulk in the shadows and hide behind the guise of a decrepit old mage.

I wished I'd had the foresight to record the conversation I'd eavesdropped on between Gelisia and Mina's relatives. What I'd overheard was more than enough to prove Gelisia was corrupt, but it was merely my word against hers, and she already held the Chief Mage's favor. I wondered how often Gelisia had taken bribes to look the other way when she had worked in my office —I had the feeling the answer was quite often; for all I knew, her subordinates delivered a part of their own take to her in exchange for her protection. Likely she would evaluate whether the victim in question possessed something worth the risk of squeezing him, and those who were too poor she did not bother with.

A flash of anger filled me at that. If I'd found out Gelisia had a "fund" such as the one she'd described to the Cantorins, I would have had her fired and indicted immediately. I was certain that if the Chief Mage of Innarta knew about this "charity" she'd set up, and that she was using it to solicit donations from people she was supposed to be investigating, that he would feel similarly. That the uncle had offered a donation at all, without her prompting, told me it was general local practice, or that he'd already heard she was amenable to bribes.

Regardless, I refused to allow Gelisia to sell off Mina's inheritance for her own profit.

"More invitations?" I asked Mina as she came into the restaurant to join me for breakfast, holding a selection of envelopes. My breath caught at the sight of her—she was wearing a sheer, multi-hued dress. Beneath it, I could clearly see the outline of her bikini. She'd been delighted when I'd suggested spending the rest of the week at the beach and had immediately proceeded to buy several bathing suits, each of which looked more enticing than the last.

The other men at the resort thought so too, and every time one of them turned his avid gaze her way, a surge of possessiveness filled me. I had to resist the temptation to growl at them since I was supposed to be a mage rather than a shifter.

"Yes, several of the people I met at Troina's party have invited me to other events," she replied, sitting down at the table. "And I'm not going to accept a single one." She regarded the stack of assorted-colored envelopes, all made of expensive linen paper. "I'd prefer to tear them up, unopened, but my grandmother's ghost would rise and haunt me if I did not at least send brief responses." She tucked them into her handbag. "It's been a while, but she did drum proper manners into me."

"Perhaps you should accept at least one or two," I suggested. "You ought to meet mages your own age, make friends among your own generation."

"Why? Do you want to get rid of me already?" Mina's eyes sparkled dangerously. "You keep saying that I should meet other people, but the mages I met at that party, while amusing for an hour or two, were boring and two-dimensional. They see me as nothing but an exotic creature, a prize, and perhaps a source of wealth." Her expression softened. "Please don't push me away, Fenris. Not now. I need you."

My defenses crumbled at the quiet desperation in her voice. "It is impossible to deny you anything when you show up to breakfast practically naked," I said wryly, trying to lighten the mood a bit. But as my eyes trailed over her form again, heat ignited inside me, awakening the hunger that always simmered when she was nearby. It would be so easy to make her clothing disappear, if only we weren't in a public place...

Mina licked her lips, her body reacting to the look in my eyes. I watched hungrily as her nipples pebbled beneath her cover-up, and my nostrils flared instinctively as I scented her arousal.

And that, of course, was when the waiter showed up.

The two of us enjoyed a hearty breakfast before heading down the short path to the hotel's secluded beach. It was mostly empty, as our fellow guests seemed to prefer the landscaped swimming pool with its floating bar.

Ducking into the bathroom, I changed into a younger, more dashing version of the old mage, with salt-and-pepper hair and a trimmed beard. Mina's eyes sparkled as I emerged in a pair of swimming trunks and sandals, her lips twitching with laughter.

"Much improved," she told me, skimming her hands down my shoulders and sides as if she were conducting an inspection, "though I still prefer you in your natural state."

Grabbing my hand, she dragged me out to the beach and straight into the water, which was pleasantly warm. Soon, we were up to our necks in it, swimming lazily in the gentle currents. Mina was like a fish—her strokes were powerful, and she could propel herself easily through the water.

"You're a very good swimmer," I told her as we floated on our backs, taking a moment to rest. "Did you go to the beach often as a child?"

Mina nodded. "I've never been to this particular resort, but my parents loved the beach, and my father taught me how to swim at an early age." Her eyes glimmered briefly with sadness, but the emotion was quickly wiped away, replaced with a fond smile. "I have many pleasant memories of the sea."

"We can make some more," I suggested, drifting over to where she was. Her skin sparkled in the sunlight, her golden hair floated in the water, and, with the way her face glowed, she looked like some sort of water goddess waiting to be worshipped.

And I was more than happy to oblige.

I took her in my arms and glided my hands over her smooth skin beneath the water, savoring the feel of her slim curves. Her eyes gleamed, and she leaned into me with a sly smile. But just when I thought she was about to kiss me, she jumped back and splashed me.

"Do you think I'm going to make it that easy?" She laughed as I sputtered. "You'll have to work for it this time, Fenris. Catch me if you can!"

She dove into the water, sleek as a seal, and my wolfish instincts roared forth at the prospect of a chase. Grinning, I swam after her, my muscled body easily cutting through the water. In seconds, I'd caught up to Mina, but before I could grab her, she spun around and splashed me again. Laughing, I splashed her back, and we were soon embroiled in an epic water fight the likes of which I hadn't participated in since I was a small child.

As Mina tried to splash me again, I ducked beneath the wave of incoming water, then propelled myself forward. She shrieked as I grabbed her by the waist, and I popped up, lifting her high. Her face was bright with laughter as I settled her onto my hips, but her eyes darkened with desire as I pressed her body close against mine. Wrapping her legs around me, she brought her core flush against my body, and I sucked in a sharp breath.

"You caught me," she said, threading her fingers through my wet hair.

"I did."

Cupping her face, I kissed her, long and slow and deep. The waves lapping against our bodies, and the faint call of seagulls, were the only sounds aside from our breathing as we stood there in the ocean, clinging to each other like life rafts. Mina moaned into my mouth, and I hardened in response, a surge of lust filling me until all I could think of was how good her curves felt pressed against my body and how much I wanted to be inside her.

When we'd made love before, I had mostly focused on her pleasure and had not taken things all the way. I'd held back out of the notion that Mina might find someone else—an absurd notion, now that I thought about it. Mina had been completely sincere this morning when she told me how she'd felt, and as a woman who had been forced into independence at a young age, who had needed to grow up quicker than most, it was only natural she would find men her own age to be shallow and lacking.

Perhaps I wasn't the perfect match for her. But I couldn't deny the feelings raging through my heart right now as I held her in my arms.

I was in love with her.

"If we keep this up, my clothing might just combust," Mina gasped, finally pulling away. Droplets of water clung to her eyelashes as she blinked up at me, her lips swollen from my kisses.

"In the water?" I teased. "That would be impressive indeed."

She laughed, the sound melodious, and I realized I wanted to hear that laugh again and again for the rest of my life. Hand in hand, we left the water, then grabbed some towels so we could dry off and toast in the sun for a while.

By the time we returned to the resort, hungry for lunch, Mina had already developed a slight tan, and I could have sworn her hair had lightened. We stopped by our rooms to shower and change, and Mina emerged in a flowing, gauzy dress the colors of sunrise. It had been all too tempting to drag her back to our rooms and strip that dress right off her, but hunger clawed at me, and I decided sex would be much better once our stomachs were sated. Sometimes my shifter need for constant fuel was a nuisance.

"Mmm," Mina said as she swallowed her first spoonful of

clam chowder. "This is delicious. It's been ages since I've eaten food like this, you know."

I nodded. "There's not much seafood in Abbsville—that I have seen, at least."

"The inn serves trout, which is plentiful in the nearby lakes, but not much else. Certainly not clams."

I opened my mouth to tell her that back in Solantha, we'd never had that problem—as a port city, seafood of all kinds was plentiful. But was I ready to tell her about my past and where I'd come from, when I hadn't even confessed my feelings to her yet?

Before I could make up my mind, Mina's face turned white, and she doubled over with a muffled groan.

"What is the matter?" I asked, alarmed at her posture and grimace of pain.

"My stomach," she moaned, squeezing her eyes shut as she clutched at her abdomen. "It hurts!"

My own stomach dropped into my shoes as horror filled me. How had this happened? The waiter immediately rushed over. "Miss, are you all right? Do I need to call a doctor?"

I snatched up the bowl of soup Mina had been enjoying and sniffed at it. The rich liquid had masked it, but this close, I could smell a faint acrid odor wafting from the soup that I recognized from my alchemy days.

"Croialis," I snapped, shooting to my feet. The colorless tincture was not susceptible to magical healing, nor would my protection spell do any good once Mina had ingested it. "She's been poisoned."

"What?" The waiter's face turned nearly as white as Mina's, and he staggered back. "How is that possible?"

"No time," I said, gathering Mina into my arms. Her eyes were still closed, and my heart clenched at the tiny moans of pain she was making. Small beads of sweat gathered on her sun-kissed brow. "Is there somewhere she can lie down?"

Shaken, the waiter led me to the office of the restaurant manager, who looked inclined to protest until he saw the state Mina was in. "I'll call for an ambulance," he said, sounding very concerned as he snatched up the phone.

I let him do it even though I knew a local doctor would be highly unlikely to be familiar with this rare poison. Even I had not come across it in over a century, and was racking my brains —was there an antidote?

"Shh," I murmured to Mina as I gently laid her down on the couch. She was trembling from head to foot, burning up with fever.

"You need to go and find out who has been messing around in your kitchen," I growled at the manager, who was standing uselessly behind me, wringing his hands. "Someone poisoned Miss Marton through your chowder. They must not be allowed to get away with this. The enforcers need to be called."

"The chowder?" The manager's eyes went wide. "That's ridiculous. Nobody touches the food but my chefs!"

"Then you had better go and talk to your chefs right away, before I take matters into my own hands."

I leveled a ferocious glare at the manager, who gulped and rushed out of the room, presumably to do as I'd commanded. Turning back to Mina, I used a spell to cool her down, thinking hard about what to do next. Croialis was a rare and extremely dangerous alkaloid derived from the seed of a tropical plant. It killed within eight hours due to liver and kidney failure. Because it could not be cured by magic, it had been used to assassinate a number of historic personages. But I remembered from my studies of history that one or two had survived the attempt—so there had to be an antidote. I had to believe that, or I would lose my mind.

If Mina did not get the antidote soon, there would be irreversible damage. If she did not get it within the eight-hour period, she would die.

If only I had access to the Solantha library with its vast collection of medical texts... my thoughts trailed off as my gaze landed on the manager's phone. Jumping up, I rushed over to the desk and snatched the phone off its cradle, then called long distance to Solantha Palace.

I dialed Iannis's office phone directly, but no one picked up, so I tried Dira, the Mages Guild receptionist, instead.

"This is Fenris."

"Fenris?" She sounded astonished. "You...you aren't dead?"

"No," I growled. "Dira, I don't have time to chat or give explanations. Please connect me to the Chief Mage, whatever he may be doing. It is a matter of life and death that I talk to him right away."

"He's in the palace," she said, "but I am not sure exactly where. Please wait."

As the minutes ticked by, a cold sweat broke out across my forehead. Was Dira really contacting Iannis, or was she alerting someone else, perhaps Director Toring? Was this phone call a giant mistake?

It's worth the risk. Whatever I have to do to save Mina's life...it's worth it.

"Fenris?" Iannis exclaimed on the other line at last. "Is it really you?"

"Yes!" Relief flooded me at the sound of my old friend's voice. "Thank Resinah I was able to reach you."

"Why in Recca haven't you called before now?" Iannis demanded. "Sunaya and I eventually figured out you were alive, but that was months ago, and—"

"I'm sorry, Iannis, but there's no time," I interrupted. "The woman I love is dying on the sofa behind me, and I need your help. Do you know an antidote for Croialis?"

I described the symptoms Mina was experiencing, along with the scent I'd identified when sniffing Mina's soup. "That certainly sounds like Croialis," he said, all business now. "I believe I know the antidote by heart, but since we cannot afford a mistake, let me run up to the library and double-check."

Iannis put me on hold for a few more minutes, then came back on the line. "You need four grams of powdered nimroot, six glowblossom petals, and two redcap mushrooms," Iannis recited. He reeled off exact instructions for how to mix the ingredients, and I scribbled them down using a pen and notepad lying on the desk. "You should be able to find these ingredients in any large apothecary."

"Thank you," I said fervently. "I promise I will call again when this is all over, and we'll catch up."

"You had better," Iannis warned. "Sunaya will have my hide when she finds out that you called and I didn't fetch her immediately. You're invited to the wedding, by the way, and we look forward to meeting your lady, once she pulls through this."

"She should, thanks to you."

I bid Iannis goodbye just as the door opened and the manager came in, a bucket of wet cloths in his hand.

"Have you found anything out from the kitchens?" I asked, taking the bucket so I could press one of the cloths to Mina's steaming forehead.

"A stranger came by to congratulate my chef on the sea bass," the manager said tightly, his eyes glimmering with anger. "My chef said it would have been easy for the man to slip a few drops of poison into the soup—your young lady's tray was sitting right there, ready to be served. The authorities have been notified, and they are searching for the fellow now."

"Did the chef give a description of the man?"

"Tall, gray hair, lanky, wearing a suit."

I gritted my teeth. That could describe any number of

people, and if it was a mage, it was likely they were in disguise anyway. "Thank you," I said, scooping Mina into my arms. "I'll take it from here."

"The ambulance hasn't gotten here yet!" the manager cried as I raced out of the room. Ignoring him, I sprinted to the front of the hotel and had the valet bring around the steamcar I'd rented. Hurriedly, I stuffed Mina into the front seat and buckled her in, then drove like a fiend into Haralis. I'd seen an apothecary in the mages quarter only a few blocks from our previous hotel, and I fervently hoped it stocked the items I needed.

It only took fifteen minutes to get to the apothecary—a quaint gray building with diamond-paned windows—but by the time we reached it, Mina's fever was back. She tossed and turned in the seat, moaning as sweat dripped down her skin and soaked through her dress.

I stopped the car in front of the apothecary, ignoring a street sign that prohibited parking. "Hang on," I murmured, brushing a kiss against her scalding forehead. "You'll be back to health in no time."

She mumbled something unintelligible, her eyelashes fluttering. I wasn't even sure she'd understood me.

I quickly put a strong protection ward on the car. With Mina inside, the last thing I needed was some thief or traffic warden absconding with her while I got the medicine. Satisfied that the ward would hold, I rushed inside, elbowing several customers out of the way.

"I need you to mix an antidote for Croialis," I said, slapping the recipe down on the counter. "*Immediately.*"

The alchemist raised her eyebrows behind her silver-rimmed glasses and looked down her nose at me. "You'll have to wait your turn like everyone else," she said, gesturing to the five people lined up, several of whom were glaring daggers at me.

I bared my teeth at her. "A woman is dying in the car right

outside here," I said in a heated voice. "Do you wish to have her death on your conscience?"

The alchemist's cheeks turned bright pink, and she recoiled in alarm. "You didn't tell me she was right outside—"

"What part of *immediately* did you not understand?" I snapped. "If she dies because of your delay or any mistake in preparing the mixture, I shall hold you accountable!"

Stiff-backed and muttering indignantly under her breath, the alchemist turned on her heel and stalked into the back of the shop, hopefully to gather ingredients. Several of the customers were edging away, toward the exit. None of them dared object to my highhandedness.

Gripping the edge of the counter, I forced myself to take several deep breaths. It was unusual for me to lash out in this way, but the thought of Mina suffering in the car for any longer than necessary simply because this woman was a stickler for the rules... I was glad I was wearing my mage disguise, or I would likely be gouging my claws into the counter at this very moment.

Fifteen minutes later, the woman marched back with a green glass bottle clutched in her bony fist. "That will be five gold coins," she said icily, handing it over.

I paid the exorbitant amount of money and snatched the bottle from the counter. "This had better be the best antidote you've ever made, or I *will* be back."

Not waiting for her response, I ran back out to the car to administer the cure. "Here," I said gently, coaxing Mina's mouth open. "Drink this. It will help you feel better."

Mina groaned, half delirious, but she did her best to swallow as I poured some of the antidote down her throat. She mumbled something that sounded very much like "tastes like cattle piss," but thankfully she didn't spit it out.

Over the next ten minutes, I gradually got her to drink more of the antidote, until half the liquid was gone. The alchemist had given me enough for two doses, so I corked the bottle and sat back with a sigh. Mina's fever had subsided, and she was sleeping peacefully in her seat, her chest rising and falling with even breaths. There was no sign of the tremors she'd been experiencing earlier.

Thank the Lady. I sagged in my seat as a wave of relief washed over me. *And Iannis.* I would have to thank him profusely the next time we spoke. Shaken by the ordeal, I gave myself a few minutes to recover, then drove back to the beachside hotel. The same valet who had helped me out was waiting for me. When I got out of the car, he anxiously asked if Mina was okay and if we needed anything. The staff seemed greatly relieved that Mina was better. Everyone was rattled by the experience—they had never seen anything like this happen before. The manager promised us free meals in the restaurant to make up for the ordeal.

I'll be sniffing every meal Mina eats until we've left Haralis, I told myself as I carefully laid Mina down onto my bed. Exhausted, I curled atop the comforter with her, spooning her from behind. Her lavender-and-sunshine scent calmed me instantly, and I closed my eyes and slipped into a much-needed nap.

———

I AWOKE a couple of hours later, my stomach growling, but I checked on Mina first. She was still fast asleep, breathing deeply. I watched her for a minute or two in the dim light, then, reassured she was recovering well, placed a strong ward on the room and left to make a quick phone call.

On my way to the lobby, I passed by the restaurant, and the scent of roasting meat nearly made me detour. But I didn't want to keep Mina waiting for long, and I could always order room service later.

To my relief, the lobby telephone had its own booth, providing me privacy and ensuring the front desk staff would not overhear. Sitting down on the small stool, I dialed Iannis's private number, then waited.

"Fenris!" Iannis exclaimed as he answered the phone so quickly I suspected he'd been waiting for it to ring. "Is everything all right? Did the antidote work?"

"By Magorah, it's really him," Sunaya exclaimed in the background, and I nearly laughed. "Damn you, Fenris, for worrying us like this! Are you okay?"

"Yes, I'm fine, and yes, the antidote worked," I told them, knowing Sunaya could hear me perfectly well. "I owe you a great debt, Iannis—Mina would have died today if not for you. I'm sorry I cut you off earlier, but time was of the essence."

"I understand completely," Iannis assured me. "You owe me no debt, Fenris—you have helped me more times than I can count. I am only glad that you and your lady love are safe."

"Speaking of lady loves," Sunaya said, and she must have grabbed the phone for her voice came through loud and clear, "you've got to bring her to our wedding, Fenris. I don't care what we have to do to make it happen—I want you to be there. I *miss* you."

The emotion in her voice triggered an answering longing in me, and I tightened my grip on the phone. "I miss you both, too, but I don't want to put you in any danger—"

"You won't be," Sunaya insisted, "and I don't want to hear any excuses. Give me your address so I can send you a formal invitation under whatever alias you're using."

I laughed, shaking my head. "I'll get one from you in person, if I decide to go," I said, though I very much doubted I would. The risk was far too great, and I was unwilling to expose Mina to any danger. Returning to Solantha, even in disguise, while the entire Convention was milling around the place, seemed like a spectacularly bad idea. "If I end up unable to make it, you know that my thoughts and wishes are with you both."

"What happened with the poison?" Iannis asked, wresting the phone from Sunaya. "Have you found out who is responsible? Croialis is not something that one could take by accident."

"We have suspicions, but no proof yet," I told him. "A large fortune is at stake, and greed is likely the motive."

"I know you can't tell us exactly where you are," Sunaya said from the background, "but are you in any immediate danger?"

"No," I assured her. "Mina is the target, not me. I will be taking extra precautions to ensure her safety, and we will be leaving here as soon as we've finished our business. I'll let you know where I settle permanently when it's safe to do so."

"Fine," she said, "but please, promise to stay in touch. I don't think we could handle it if you did another disappearing act."

I smiled. "I'll do my best."

When I finally hung up the phone, I felt more at peace than I had in months. Hearing Iannis and Sunaya on the phone had soothed the ache of homesickness inside me, and I was glad that they were not very angry with me for misleading them. No matter how great the distance, or how long we were out of contact, our friendship had remained solid.

Satisfied, I headed back to the room to order food and keep my vigil with Mina.

———

"Fenris?"

Mina's groggy voice woke me from my nap at her side, and I opened my eyes to see the sunset filtering in through the blinds.

"Are you all right?" I asked, sitting up so I could turn her onto her back. Mina's eyelids were heavy with sleep, and there was a look of confusion on her face. But there was healthy color in her cheeks, and no sign of pain or distress.

"I...I think so." She blinked a few times to clear her vision. "What happened?"

"Someone poisoned your soup," I said, brushing a lock of golden hair off her face. Touching Mina was soothing—it reminded me that she was still alive, still with me. Wanting more of that touch, I gathered her in my arms and pressed my lips against her forehead. "It was Croialis, a rare poison made of a tropical seed that kills within hours. Thank the Lady I recognized the smell and was able to get you the antidote in time. I don't know what I would have done if I'd lost you."

"Thank you for saving me." Mina's hand gently stroked down my back, and it occurred to me that it was a little absurd that she was the one comforting me. But I needed it, I silently admitted as I held her tightly. The thought of her lying dead and cold on the ground, robbed of the centuries of life she had yet to look forward to... I couldn't bear the idea. I would do anything to make sure she was safe.

Anything.

"Fenris..." Mina trailed off, her voice hesitant.

I pulled back a little to scan her expression. "What is it?"

She searched my face, her fingers feathering across my bearded jaw. "It's just...you thanked the Lady, Resinah, instead of Magorah, the way other shifters do. And you know so many things about magic, poisons, politics, and law.... Don't you trust me enough by now to explain why you are so different from other shifters? So unique?"

I sighed, figuring now was as good a time as any to tell her the truth, so I conjured the privacy bubble. I might confide my dangerous secrets to Mina, but hardly to the hotel staff. "It's not that I did not trust you, Mina, but sharing my secrets could be dangerous to you."

"I don't care. Ignorance is worse than danger, Fenris. I'm not a child who needs to be shielded from the truth." She regarded me steadily out of those pretty silver-gray eyes. I supposed I would have felt the same in her position.

"Very well, then." I took a deep breath, a little nervous how she would react to my revelations. "My original given name was Polar ar'Tollis," I told her. "I was born into a mage family, just like you, and completed my apprenticeship long ago. I was Chief Mage of Nebara, once upon a time." It was only four years ago, but it seemed another lifetime. *Was* another lifetime, as I was a different man now.

"A *Chief Mage*?" Mina stared at me, wide-eyed. "How is that possible? There has never been a shifter chief mage, or even I would have heard."

I chuckled at that idea. "Of course not. I was a full-blooded mage at the time, with a quite different face. As Lord Polar, I led a life similar to that of any other chief mages, creating gold, administering my state, and so on."

Mina's brow furrowed, as if she was chasing an elusive memory. "That name, Lord Polar. It sounds familiar somehow, but I'm not sure why."

I laughed a little. "I forget that you have been so isolated from mage politics and gossip," I said. "I saved the life of a human girl who was to be executed. For that transgression, I was convicted of high treason. I was forced to flee Nebara or be executed myself. There was a Federation-wide manhunt. Actually, there still is, though it has mostly died down."

Mina shook her head, her eyes wide. "Why was the girl going to be executed?"

"She was a wild talent and had a run-in with a mage official." I did not mention that when I first realized Mina had magic, I had been afraid she might be in similar danger. Thankfully, her parentage protected her from that at least.

"I want to know it all," Mina said, scooting closer to me. She cupped my cheek, searching my face with those gentle eyes. "Tell me the story of how a mage became a shifter."

I took a deep breath, then told her the story of Polar ar'Tollis, and how he had come to be Fenris, the man she knew today.

How I'd buried myself in my duties and scholarly pursuits, devoting my spare time into studying all forms of magic, its history, and its development.

How I'd never once looked outside my ivory tower at the conditions humans and mages dealt with, until I was suddenly staring at the execution order of a little girl waiting for my seal and signature.

How, faced with death, I had allowed a good friend to experiment on me with an ancient and highly illegal transformation spell, fully expecting to die.

Except I hadn't died. And when I'd awoken in my new form as a wolf shifter, I'd discovered I still retained some of my magic, though much less than before.

"No wonder you are such an odd shifter," Mina said when I was finished. "You are really a mage underneath! Wow, if Marris or Barrla had any idea ...." She stared at me as though she were seeing me for the first time. "What was it like to be suddenly a shifter, after all that time as a mage? It must have been very disorienting."

"You could say that," I agreed. "I had no idea that the wolf who joined me in body and mind would produce such a drastic change in me. Not only my body and senses, but also my feelings and priorities have changed. Overall, for the better. At first, I had a tough time coming to terms with what I had become, since I shared the usual mage disdain for lesser races. But I have made my peace with it. In fact, I rather prefer Fenris to the man I used to be."

"But you still have so many of Polar's traits—his love for

books and reading, his knowledge of the law, of politics, and so on." Mina grinned. "Apart from the loss of magical strength, I would say you got the best of both worlds."

"Perhaps," I agreed. "My decades of study are the reason I know so many spells, but my reduced magical strength is why I need your help to use some of them. You have significantly more power than me, though not quite as much as I used to wield before my transformation." I did not bother to mention that my powers seemed to be slowly recovering, perhaps through frequent use.

"What a strange story," Mina murmured. "But it explains so much."

She traced the bones of my face with her fingertips, and I dropped the illusion so she could see me as I really was—as I always would be. I could wear various disguises, but never again would I be Polar ar'Tollis, the foolish Chief Mage who'd kept his head buried in the sand until it was too late. My eyes were wide open now, and perhaps they saw too much at times.

But right now, I was looking at exactly what I wanted to see.

"Do you understand now why I was so hesitant about getting involved with you?" I asked. "I will forever be a wanted man, Mina. There is no real future for me."

"I doubt that very much," Mina said wryly. "You are a brilliant man, Fenris, and you've still got many years of life ahead of you, as do I. How old are you, anyway?"

"One hundred and seventy-six."

Mina's eyes flew wide in mock-surprise. "Over one-seventy! You really *are* an old man." She pretended to push me away, then giggled when I growled and pulled her back against me. "You certainly don't have the stamina of an old man," she teased as I nuzzled her neck.

"True, and thank the Lady for that."

I kissed her, and we spent several minutes touching and

stroking and tasting each other. But Mina was still drained from her near-death experience, so I buried my lust and tucked her in against my chest so we could drift off to sleep again.

There would be plenty of time for lovemaking and celebration once we got through the hearing tomorrow.

20

MINA

The next morning, Fenris and I rose bright and early to get ready for our hearing with the Chief Mage. I was grateful to feel mostly normal after a deep sleep—the near-fatal poisoning had shown me how uncertain even a mage's long life could be.

Feeling refreshed, I dressed in one of the elegant new outfits I'd bought the day I'd run into Troina—a robin's egg blue gown with bell sleeves and a skirt that flared out at the waist. I dressed my hair with opal clips I'd picked up at a jeweler a few doors down from the dressmaker's and put on the ivory-colored slippers that matched the shimmering thread shot through the fabric of the skirt.

By the time I'd finished dressing, I felt as if I were going to war.

"All ready?" Fenris asked as he met me in the hall. He was back in his old-mage guise, and his eyes gleamed with admiration as he looked me up and down. "You look perfect."

"Thank you." I tried for a smile, but my stomach was a bundle of nerves. Fenris seemed to understand, because he didn't press me to eat breakfast—he simply ordered a glass of freshly pressed orange juice for me, which he carefully sniffed before he let me drink. Soon enough, we were in the steamcar and headed into the city.

"You'll be fine," Fenris assured me as we pulled up to Haralis Palace. My stomach was dancing a frenetic tune, and I felt as if it were going to jump out of my throat. "Gelisia will do her worst, but she cannot break you. She is not all-powerful, and you have the truth on your side."

Nodding, I swallowed hard, then gathered my composure as we stepped from the cab. Holding my head high, I glided up the steps like royalty, then announced to the receptionist that I was there for my hearing with the Chief Mage. Fenris and I were escorted back, not to the waiting room where we'd been before but to the formal audience chamber.

The audience chamber was a cavernous hall with vaulted ceilings and ornate tapestries decorated with glittering gold runes. A carpet ran the length of the burnished gold floor, and at the end, on a raised platform, sat a throne-like chair. On either side of it were two smaller chairs, and below the platform sat a desk, where a typewriter would be used to transcribe the hearing. The room was entirely empty, and Fenris and I took up spots to the left of the dais to wait.

It wasn't long before the hall door opened again and my relatives trooped in, along with the family lawyer. Mr. Ransome's expression was carefully blank, while my uncle and cousin looked faintly smug, almost triumphant. The lawyer greeted me cordially as they passed, though the rest of them said nothing. I could have sworn I caught a glimpse of something like guilt in my aunt's eyes, but when I met her gaze, she was stone-faced. I turned away, annoyed I'd entertained, for even one moment, the hope that she might feel sympathy for me.

These people were related to me in name only. I felt no

kinship with them whatsoever, and once I was through with this hearing, I would never speak to them again.

Finally, a side door opened, and the Chief Mage and Miss Dorax strode into the room along with some underlings, one of whom took a seat at the stenographer's desk. Everyone stood and bowed as the Chief Mage stepped onto the dais, and I lifted my head as he took the central seat to preside over the hearing.

"Is everyone accounted for?" he asked Miss Dorax, who sat at his right, leaving the left chair empty.

Miss Dorax's dark eyes swept the room. "It would appear so," she said in that smoky voice of hers. "Are you ready to begin, my lord?"

"Yes. Please present your report."

I held my breath as Gelisia pulled a sheaf of papers from the sleeve of her robe—most mages kept a magical pocket there that could store an almost infinite number of items. "In the interest of brevity, let me go straight to the summary. I have interviewed both parties and several witnesses. Based on all pertinent evidence, my conclusion is that the young lady presenting herself as Tamina Marton has failed to present convincing proof of her identity."

Heat began to rise to my cheeks as she smiled faintly, and I had to force my anger back. "She does bear a remarkable resemblance to the late Miss Marton that has managed to fool some of the real Tamina's former friends. However, they have not seen her since she was a mere child, so little weight can be given to their impressions. To an unbiased observer, it is evident the real Tamina Marton perished in the sea at age fifteen, as the investigation at the time concluded. I see no reason why its result should now be overturned. This imposter before us should be punished for trying to steal another family's fortune by her bold imposture and fined the entire cost of the proceedings."

The smug looks on Uncle Bobb and Vanley's faces grew into

smirks. This time, I allowed my hands to clench into fists. "Well?" the Chief Mage asked them, looking faintly bored. I realized he must have already read the written report and had anticipated what Gelisia was going to announce. This was all just a formality.

"We fully concur with Miss Dorax's findings," my uncle said. "While this imposter does bear some resemblance to our dear Tamina, she has nothing of her character. This woman's claims are an insult to my niece's memory."

That guilty look crossed my aunt's face again, but she did nothing to contradict my uncle. I felt another flash of searing anger.

"May I please speak, Lord Zaran?" I asked, forcing myself to remain calm.

He gave me a long look. "Yes," he finally said, and I stepped forward.

"The conclusion presented by your financial secretary is ludicrous. Her interview of me took place in a restaurant, and she barely seemed interested in the evidence I tried to offer." I turned and gave my relatives a scathing look. "Two of these people might be my relatives by blood, but they are not my family," I said with feeling. "I did not go out swimming that night, nor did I drown. The only witness to that is Vanley, who has every reason to lie about it. He cornered me in the hall when I left my room to get a glass of milk from the kitchen and was threatening to rape me." My voice trembled a little, and out of the corner of my eye, I saw my aunt's face pale. "I lashed out with my magic to send him tumbling down the stairs, then ran away from the house in desperation, because my aunt and uncle had refused to protect me from months of harassment and violence at Vanley's hands. Given that record, the Cantorin family does not deserve a single copper of the Marton fortune.

My parents and grandmother would turn over in their graves at such blatant injustice."

"That's preposterous," my uncle sneered. "My son would never have laid a hand on Tamina. He was a pious boy, too focused on his studies to bother with girls. I refuse to listen to such baseless accusations."

"Lord Zaran," Fenris said calmly before the Chief Mage could respond. "While I cannot speak to what happened here in Haralis thirteen years ago, I witnessed Miss Dorax meeting with the Cantorin family and soliciting a bribe in exchange for framing Miss Marton as an imposter. You may not be aware of it, but your financial secretary has a history of unethical behavior."

Gelisia's face turned white with fury, and the Chief Mage's eyes widened with incredulous anger. "You dare slander a member of my office?" he asked, and the air around him crackled with power. "Without any proof but your unsupported word?"

I flinched at the force of the Chief Mage's ire—I couldn't help it—but Fenris stood his ground, appearing unruffled by the outburst. "All of this could easily be cleared up with a truth wand. I believe that in most states of the Federation, it is customary to consult one in such contentious cases. The process is simple and painless—why not send for a wand to double-check everyone's claims rather than relying blindly on subordinates?"

Fenris then proceeded to cite several historic cases where a truth wand uncovered who had really been lying or revealed that key officials were covering up certain details to sway the outcome of cases one way or another. The Chief Mage listened quietly, but even so, I could tell he wasn't thrilled by the suggestion of questioning everyone with a wand—no doubt he was displeased that Fenris was calling the integrity of his office into question. Still, that he listened at all gave me a tiny sliver of hope.

"That is all well and good, but it is not customary to engage a truth wand here in Innarta," Gelisia snapped the moment Fenris stopped talking. "We will not be using one for this case."

"Miss Dorax," the Chief Mage said sharply. "I believe that is my call to make, not yours."

Gelisia's cheeks flushed, and she bowed. "Of course, my lord."

The Chief Mage was silent for a long moment, and I could tell he was fighting an internal battle. Part of him did not want to use the truth wand because that would admit to a weakness in his office and error in his conclusions. But the other part of him, his pride, could not bear one of his subordinates dictating how this hearing would be conducted. In her arrogance, Gelisia had overreached.

"Very well," he finally said. "Send for the truth wand."

One of the underlings bowed before rushing from the room. A nervous silence descended upon the hall, and everyone except Fenris and the Chief Mage looked uncomfortable. Even Miss Dorax seemed distressed, her pouty lips pressed in a thin line. I felt a smug satisfaction as I looked at her. *I* didn't have anything to fear from the truth wand—all I needed to do was repeat what I'd said earlier.

The side door creaked open a few minutes later, and the underling came back in, along with an elderly librarian who carried a rectangular lacquered case. He presented the case to the Chief Mage, who opened it and removed a slender wand carved from beech. It shimmered faintly in the light, and I glimpsed the intricate runes carved into it that swirled around the length of polished wood.

"Tamina Marton," the Chief Mage said gravely, "please step forward."

I did, standing very still as the Chief Mage waved his wand. A shower of sparks descended onto me, and my skin glowed faintly blue. "Answer my questions truthfully, and nothing will change," he said. "Lie, and the light around you will turn red, exposing your falsehood."

I nodded, proceeding to answer the Chief Mage's questions, repeating everything I'd said earlier, starting with my name and parentage. He prodded me for more information at certain points, asking me how long the abuse had occurred, whether I'd sought help, and so on. I worried he might force me to reveal where I'd been, or Fenris's true identity, but to my relief, his questions never veered in that direction.

"The wand has verified that everything Miss Marton states is true, and that she is who she says she is," the Chief Mage said sternly. He turned his gaze to my relatives. "Is there anything about her statement you'd like to refute?"

I turned to look at my aunt and uncle, who shook their heads. Uncle Bobb and Vanley looked murderous, and they glared daggers at me, but my aunt seemed almost relieved. I felt a little more warmly to her. Yes, she'd been too cowardly to stand up for me, but for all I knew, my uncle was just as much of an abuser as Vanley had been.

"Very well. Miss Dorax, step up."

"My lord..." Gelisia began in a conciliatory tone, but trailed off at the frozen look on the Chief Mage's face. He already knew she'd lied—there was no convincing him of her innocence. Now it only remained for him to uncover the depth of her corruption.

The Chief Mage waved the wand, showering her with sparks as he'd done with me. "Is it true, Miss Dorax, that you met with the Cantorin family this past week with the intention of solic-iting a bribe from them?"

"I—" Gelisia began, then clammed up as the glow around

her turned a dark, ugly red. "Yes," she hissed through her teeth, fisting her hands at her sides.

"I see," the Chief Mage said coldly. "And did you, in fact, solicit a bribe from Mr. Cantorin in exchange for slanting the investigation in his favor?"

"I solicited contributions to the Dorax Fund," Gelisia answered, her tone equally cold. "A non-profit organization set up to help indigent students."

"Do not treat me like a fool, Miss Dorax," the Chief Mage said, his eyes flat. "I know very well how both mages and humans alike use 'non-profits' to funnel gold through, and I suspect a forensic accountant will reveal that your charity is not above board." He shook his head, looking deeply disappointed. "I am ashamed to have allowed this to happen right beneath my nose. You are suspended, Miss Dorax, pending further disciplinary action, and you are ordered not to leave Haralis until further notice."

Gelisia tried to protest, but the Chief Mage refused to hear another word. She spun on her heel and flounced out of the room in a towering fury. As Fenris and I watched her go, I saw a gleam of satisfaction in his eyes, and I could only imagine how good he must feel to watch Gelisia finally get the comeuppance she deserved. Hopefully she would never hold a government position again.

"Lord Zaran," Fenris said once the doors had slammed shut behind Gelisia and everything had quieted again. "There have been two attempts on Miss Marton's life recently—she was nearly run over by a steamcar last week, and yesterday, someone slipped poison into her food. It is obvious that someone has been trying to eliminate her, and in view of the Cantorin family's lies, I would ask that they be questioned about the issue while you still have the truth wand at hand."

The Chief Mage nodded, all previous signs of reluctance gone. "Mr. Cantorin, please step up."

My relatives grudgingly came before the Chief Mage and submitted themselves to the truth wand. While all of them admitted they had been lying when they'd claimed they did not recognize me as the real Tamina Marton, they swore they had no knowledge of the assassination attempts on me and had not hired anyone to carry out such a heinous crime. Fenris and I exchanged surprised looks—I had been almost certain it was one of them—but the truth wand did not detect any falsehood, and we were forced to accept their testimony.

"Very well," the Chief Mage said as he dismissed Vanley. "It is possible that these 'attempts' were mere accidents, but I shall have someone from the Enforcers Guild look into the matter."

Turning back to my relatives, he declared, "In view of your audacious lies, and your failure to properly care for Miss Marton when she was at a vulnerable age, you are hereby relieved of your guardianship of her person and responsibility as stewards of the Marton Estate. You will hand over all monies, lands, and anything else belonging to the estate within two weeks' time. You will also vacate any properties belonging to Miss Marton immediately and not seek any contact with her whatsoever in the future."

My relatives looked utterly confounded by this pronouncement, and I had to bite back an incredulous laugh. Had they really thought they would waltz out of this unscathed? If I had been them, saddled with the knowledge of my guilt, I would have been beside myself with fear. It was amazing to me that all they seemed to feel was anger, except perhaps for my aunt, who simply looked miserable. No doubt she was thinking of all the parties and cruises she would no longer be able to host or partake in.

"Miss Marton," the Chief Mage said to me, "the Mages Guild

will conduct a full inventory and an audit of the accounts before turning your inheritance over to you and your legal representatives. Given that you are not far off the age of majority and missed the training due to you by birth through no fault of your own, I hereby emancipate you—you are now considered an adult by law and no longer have need of any guardian."

"Thank you," I said with feeling, curtsying deeply. I was certain the Chief Mage had awarded me my majority out of guilt at what had very nearly been a grave miscarriage of justice, but the why of it didn't matter. I was free at long last, and a wave of giddy relief swept over me as it finally hit me that I had nothing more to fear.

"Mina," Aunt Allira pleaded, stepping forward. The guilt was plain on her face now, and she actually wrung her hands. "Please, you have to understand, I never wanted any of this—"

"That's enough," my uncle growled, pulling her back. He turned away, steering his wife toward the exit, and Vanley shot me a venomous glance over his shoulder as he followed them out.

Blaming me, rather than himself, for all of this. How typical.

"Congratulations," Mr. Ransome said to me, and I blinked—I'd nearly forgotten about him. He'd taken care to remain in the background, silent. "On reaching your majority over a year early, and for winning the case against such high odds. I'll gather all the records together as ordered—the Mages Guild will have them presently," he added to the Chief Mage.

He took his leave as well, and Fenris struck up a conversation with the Chief Mage—something about various legal precedents for punishing dishonest officials. I only half listened, my relief already giving way to a feeling of unease. Yes, I'd gotten everything I'd wanted...but someone had tried to kill me twice, and I was still no closer to discovering who that person was.

21

MINA

After Fenris finished his conversation with the Chief Mage, he whisked me out of the palace and into the warm, sunny day. "Let's celebrate," he suggested, and I was more than happy to oblige. There was no point in dwelling on the loose threads right now—I'd just scored a momentous victory, and after everything we'd been through to get here, we deserved to enjoy our triumph for a bit.

Now that my stomach was no longer a knot of nerves, I was famished—I hadn't eaten anything yet today. We quickly found a cheerful, open-air bistro, and ordered brunch and mimosas— Fenris couldn't get inebriated, but he'd told me in the past that he enjoyed the slight burn of alcohol all the same and didn't mind indulging every so often.

"Coffee has no stimulating effect on me either," he said ruefully after the waiter had delivered steaming cups for both of us. "But I spent so much of my life drinking it that I rather enjoy the morning ritual."

"Really? I didn't know that." I reached for my own cup of coffee, but Fenris tugged the mug across the table. He took a deep sniff, and my skin went cold as I realized he was checking for poison.

"All safe," he said, pushing the cup back toward me. I stared at it for a long moment before reaching for the small container of cream. "I'm sorry, Mina," he said gently, "but until we catch the killer, we have to take precautions." He proceeded to sniff the cream jug, too, before handing it back to me.

"You don't need to apologize for trying to protect me," I said as I lightened my coffee. "It's just...it's hard for me to celebrate, knowing that my life is still in danger."

"I know what you mean," Fenris said, with feeling. As I gazed into his eyes, I thought about how he'd spent the past few years living with the threat of discovery and execution always looming over his head. At least I had never had to worry about that—the worst that would have happened if I'd been caught was that I'd be forced to return to my relatives. Living on my own had hardened me enough that I probably would have been able to deal with Vanley, and even though I would have been miserable, I would have lived, at least.

The food arrived, and my stomach grumbled as the large platter was set before me—eggs, bacon, and pancakes. I was about to dig in when Fenris reached over and switched our plates.

"Hey!" I protested as he began to eat my food after a quick whiff.

"We ordered the same thing," Fenris pointed out with a raised eyebrow, and I glanced down at my new plate to see that he was right.

"That doesn't mean you should eat it," I protested. "It would be just as bad if *you* were to die instead of me."

"Shifters are immune to most poisons," he said in a low voice so no one else could hear. "And besides, I disagree. You have a long life before you, whereas I've already lived a good portion of mine. In many people's opinion, I should not even be alive today. If I were a cat," he added, his lips twitching, "I would have used up several of my nine lives already."

"As would I," I pointed out after swallowing a mouthful of pancake. "The steamcar, and the poison...perhaps even the night I ran away from Vanley." I doubted my cousin would have killed me, but any number of thugs or highway criminals could have done so during my flight—I was a young girl, traveling alone, and I'd been very lucky I hadn't been accosted.

"Now that you are a legal adult, you ought to write a will, sooner rather than later," Fenris said grimly, all pretense of enjoying the beautiful morning gone. "Until you do, your aunt is still your heir as she is your closest living relative. It would be best if you find a different lawyer for this, one who has no connection whatsoever to the Cantorin family."

I pursed my lips. "And yet, my relatives are not the ones who tried to kill me, if the truth wand is to be believed. So why is someone else trying to murder me? Who stands to profit from my death?"

Our eyes met, and we had the same thought at the same time. "The lawyer," we said simultaneously.

"Could it really be, though?" I bit my lip at the thought of Mr. Ransome being the would-be murderer—he'd acted a little funny when I'd first walked into his office but had seemed sincerely glad for me at the hearing today. "What would Mr. Ransome stand to gain from my death?"

"Well..." Fenris drummed his fingers on the table, his brow furrowed in thought. "Mr. Ransome was your trustee, and if he were a truly honest man, he would not have allowed your relatives full access to your funds before the statutory thirteen years were over. It stands to reason that he was permitting them to do so in order to feather his own nest—confident they would not dare call him to account for any losses, since they were also in the wrong."

"And now that the Mages Guild is planning to do an audit..." I murmured, my eyes going wide, "all of this will come to light, if it's true."

And Mr. Ransome's goose would be well and truly cooked.

"Penalties for dishonest lawyers and trustees are very steep," Fenris said, "starting with disbarment and going all the way up to execution, depending on the severity of the breach. Mr. Ransome has a very good reason indeed for wanting you dead."

Chills raced along my skin, raising the hair along my arms. "I'm still having trouble believing that it's him," I said, shaking my head. By the Lady, Mr. Ransome had known me since I was in pigtails, and he'd never struck me as particularly sinister, or at all dangerous. Could his heart really be so cold that he'd have no qualms about killing me?

"I know it's an unpleasant thought," Fenris said, "but until the killer is caught, we can't rule him out. In fact, now that the case has been resolved in your favor, you are in more danger than ever." He straightened in his chair, his expression grim. "Ransome only has days, or even hours, to make this go away and save his career."

Those words were like an icy bucket of water dumped straight onto my head. Fenris snapped his fingers to conjure an ether pigeon and quickly gave it a brief message to the Chief Mage. Since pigeons could not remember more than three sentences, he merely pointed out Ransome's possible motive and asked for an investigation. I blinked as the magical bird disappeared in a shower of blue sparks—I hadn't seen one of those since I was a child, as they had mostly gone out of fashion with the invention of the telephone.

After we'd finished eating, Fenris immediately herded me back to the hotel. "Until the danger is past," he vowed, his grip tight on the steering wheel, "we will stay out of harm's way. I will not allow a single hair on your head to be harmed."

"You are not going to confront Ransome yourself and knock him down?" I teased. In truth, I was glad he was not the type to act first and think later, like so many men of my acquaintance.

Fenris smiled. "I would love to do that, but we need to wait for the proof, and I'm no accountant—that is a job for professionals. In the meantime, your safety is infinitely more important than confronting the man with our suspicions."

Part of me wanted to point out that since I now was legally an adult, I was perfectly capable of deciding for myself. But in truth, it was enjoyable to have someone who I cared about be so protective. So I allowed him to take charge, not even protesting when he told me to pack my things.

"Where are we going?" I asked as I dragged my suitcase, now filled to the brim with all my extra belongings, out into the hall. "We're not leaving Innarta, are we?"

"No," Fenris said, and for the first time today, he smiled. "We're going on an island cruise."

22

FENRIS

At first, Mina had protested when I told her we were taking a short getaway. Though she still wasn't entirely convinced Ransome was responsible for the attacks on her, she claimed she wanted to be there when he was either arrested or exonerated. But I managed to convince her to leave this to the Mages Guild—a guilty mage with nothing to lose was too dangerous to face down, and we had no idea of Mr. Ransome's magical potential.

"Let the Chief Mage do his job for a change," I suggested, taking her in my arms. "It will take his accountants at least a week to scrutinize the books, after all these years. Why not enjoy ourselves in the meantime?"

And so here we are, I thought as I watched Mina stand at the prow of the yacht I'd rented. Backlit by the setting sun, she was breathtaking, her hair streaming out behind her in ribbons of gold, and the skirts of her teal sundress whipping about her lithe form like a banner.

Unable to resist, I came up and put my arms around her from behind, nuzzling her neck. She giggled a little, leaning into me. As I inhaled her sweet scent, I couldn't help but wish I could capture this moment in a bottle, so I might take it out and look at it every time I felt a little melancholy in the future. Mina was the star I looked up to every day—not a brilliantly blazing one, like Sunaya, whose fire one had to be able to withstand to get close. No, Mina's light was a gentle one, something I could follow when I was lost or just needed an anchor to ground myself with.

When I was with her, I felt like I was at home.

"I love you," I told her, pressing a kiss against her jawline.

Slowly, she turned in my arms. "I thought you might never say it," she said. She kissed me softly, a feather light touch of lips against lips that nevertheless ignited that heat inside me. "Are you done keeping me at arm's length, then?"

"Yes." I'd abandoned my old-mage guise—it was my own strong arms that wrapped around her, my own chest that rested against hers, that could feel her heartbeat fluttering behind her ribcage. "But before you tell me whether you return my feelings, let's have dinner, and I'll answer anything you want to know about me."

After I led her down to the cozy yet elegant dining area, I served up a dinner of steaks and asparagus, cooked quickly yet perfectly with a few culinary spells I'd picked up.

"I had no idea mages used magic to cook food," Mina said around a mouthful of steak. She swallowed and made a pleased noise in the back of her throat. "This is delicious."

I smiled. "Most mages don't," I told her, "but in my former life, I studied all sorts of magic. One day, I came across an old spellbook in a used bookstore that covered a range of culinary magic. I never mastered the whole thing—I had servants to take care of the cooking, after all—but I did learn enough to prepare a few favorite dishes for myself."

Mina laughed a little. "Servants," she said, shaking her head. "I forgot already that you used to be a Chief Mage."

"That man is gone, and perhaps it is for the best." I said wryly. "I bear no resemblance to the man I once was."

"Well, of course not, now that you've been changed into a shifter. That must have been scary."

I winced. "It would be better if you forgot about that part, or at least never mentioned it again." I had not told her who had saved me—what Iannis had done was highly illegal, and the fewer who knew about it, the safer he would be.

"I don't think I mentioned who precipitated my downfall, did I?"

Mina shook her head. "No, just that it was your Finance Secretary."

My lips twisted into a bitter smile. "It was Gelisia Dorax," I said, and Mina's mouth formed a small 'o' of surprise. "I told you earlier that we were acquaintances, but it was more than that— she was my Finance Secretary. It was she who found out I had let the child escape by spying on me, hoping to find some dirt on her boss. She denounced me, brought down the anger of the government on my head. She did offer to turn a blind eye if I'd marry her and then step down in her favor," I added with a scoff, "but I knew even then I'd rather die."

"No wonder you were so upset when we first saw her," Mina exclaimed. "I'm not sure I could have stood to be in her presence if I'd been in your position, knowing she was responsible for ruining your life!"

"Well," I said, lifting Mina's hand so I could press a kiss against her knuckles. "I wouldn't say my life has been ruined... merely altered. And it has brought me to you, so I can't regret it."

Mina blushed. "You are far too good to me," she said, cupping my cheek with the hand I'd kissed. "You are unique, and I'll never meet another man who will understand and support me the way you do."

"Does that mean you love me, then?" I teased, and she rose

to come and sit in my lap. My heart began to beat faster as she twined her slender arms around my neck and leaned in.

"I do, very much indeed, and I don't want you to ever again suggest that we can't be together," she declared. "We are both smart, resourceful people—if anyone can figure it out, we can."

She kissed me fiercely, and I growled into her mouth, finally letting go of my last reservations. She was mine, and I hers. My hands dove into her hair and I entangled my fingers in the silken length as I kissed her hard and deep, greedily drinking in the taste of her. The tiny noise of pleasure she made in the back of her throat stoked the flames that were building inside me, and I ached to strip her sundress off and take her right here on the table.

But that wouldn't do, not for the first time that I would take her fully.

I was just about to stand up and take her to bed when she pulled back and yanked off my tunic belt. "Off," she demanded, tugging at my clothes, and the fiery blaze of passion in her eyes made it impossible to deny her anything. Lifting my arms, I let her remove my tunic, and she began kissing her way down my chest, sinking down on her knees until she was kneeling on the floor between my legs.

"By the Lady," I groaned as she took me into her hot, silken mouth. The feel of her tongue sliding along my length was nearly enough to make me come right then and there. I fisted a hand in her hair to try to pull her away, but then she began to suck, and I couldn't make myself do it. The sight of her on her knees, with my cock in her mouth, was the most erotic thing I'd ever seen. She felt so good that I couldn't stop her if my life depended on it.

"Mmm," she said in encouragement as I subconsciously began to rock my hips into her. I tried to control my motions, not wanting to hurt her, but she dug her fingers into my rear, refusing to allow me to hold back. I surged forward, coming in her mouth with a roar so loud I was certain it could be heard from the mainland.

"I've always wondered what that would be like," Mina said with a feline smile as she pulled back. "I'll definitely have to do it again."

I shook my head, lifting her into my arms. "I didn't mean to come," I told her. "I wanted to be inside you."

Mina laughed lightly, skimming her hands along my shoulders. "I'm sure we can get you riled up again," she said, leaning in to bite my bottom lip. She wrapped her bare legs around my waist, and sure enough, I felt another surge of lust as she pressed her wet core against me.

Could I ever get enough of this woman? Did I even want to?

Abandoning the mess we'd made at dinner, I carried Mina to the captain's bedroom—small but luxurious quarters with polished hardwood flooring, a large window that opened directly onto the sea, and a soft bed that beckoned. There were blinds on the window, but I elected to leave them open—there was no one around for miles, and even if another ship did pass, the bed was positioned in such a way that they wouldn't be able to directly see us anyway.

"When I finally get myself a new house," Mina said with a sigh as I set her down onto the bed, her gaze on the window, "I want our bedroom to look out over the ocean."

Our bedroom. "Then it shall," I said before I kissed her again.

Mina wrapped her arms around me, drawing me in close as she kissed me back, soft and slow and with unspeakable tenderness. Reaching between us, I stroked between her legs until she was vibrating beneath me, my fingers soaked with the evidence of her arousal.

"Are you ready?" I asked, pulling back to look at her.

She nodded, gazing up at me out of heavy-lidded eyes that

were smoky with lust. "Take me," she breathed, spreading her legs and reaching for me. I hissed as she wrapped her fingers around my cock and gently guided me to her entrance.

"Oh," she moaned as I surged forward, burying myself in her. I groaned, pressing my face into the crook of her neck as a bolt of pleasure lanced through me. She was so tight. When she arched her hips, taking me in even deeper, I thought I might lose my mind. I bit down on the inside of my cheek to rein myself in, and the pain grounded me a little.

And then I began to move inside her.

I started off with slow, gentle strokes to get Mina used to the feel of me. She reached up to cup my face with both hands, her silver eyes shining, and my heart grew so full I feared it might burst. Leaning in, I took her mouth in another soft kiss, but she bit down on my lower lip and began undulating her hips, urging me faster.

"More," she gasped against my mouth, and I was all too happy to oblige. I reached a hand between us to stroke her in time to my thrusts, and she came almost instantly, arching her back, her hands fisted in the sheets. Her inner walls clenched around me, the last straw, and I let myself go, my own release sweeping through me with such intensity that, for a moment, I forgot where I was.

And then I came back down to reality to see Mina looking up at me with the most blissful expression on her face—an expression I was certain mirrored my own. Groaning, I collapsed on top of her, then rolled onto my side and gathered her in my arms.

"That was incredible," I said, nuzzling her shoulder.

"Yes," she agreed, turning in my arms. She ran her fingers down my chest, playing with my hair as she seemed to like to do. Her eyes sparkled as she looked up at me and said, "When are we going to do it again?"

23

MINA

One week later, I stood by the railing, watching the yacht port approach as Fenris expertly steered our ship back to Haralis. We'd had a wonderful time these past few days visiting the nearby islands, making love in the surf in secluded areas of the beach, and just enjoying each other's company in general.

Indulging in playtime hadn't been the only thing we'd done on our little vacation. Fenris had taught me several useful spells and told me more about his life—how much he missed his friends Iannis and Sunaya in Solantha since he'd left them in the confusion of the big quake before they could become further embroiled in his troubles. That his parents were still alive and had no idea what had become of him, and how eager certain officials in the capital were to make an example of the elusive Lord Polar. It was amazing how much he had been silently dealing with—but no longer. I would be by his side for all of it now.

I feel like a new woman, I thought as we docked. More experienced and sure of myself, and I wasn't just referring to my relationship with Fenris. Though that too had changed. Our intimacy had reached new heights when he'd finally let go of his reservations and made love to me completely. He'd been good with his mouth and hands, but the feel of him inside me... pleasant shivers raced through me, a blush spreading across my cheeks. I hadn't known how good sex could truly feel, not until our first night aboard the yacht.

But my sex life wasn't the only thing I was happy about. Forcing myself to face down my old demons had strengthened something in me I'd believed broken. I had not even worried about the killer these past few days. With Fenris by my side, watching out for threats, checking my food, and sharing my bed every night, there had been nothing to fear.

All that remained was to learn the results of the audit, but even that did not overly concern me. I suspected a good chunk of my fortune would be gone, but in the past thirteen years I'd grown so used to living modestly that whatever was left to me would still be far more than I needed.

"Are you ready?" Fenris asked, coming to stand by my side.

I turned to him, and a pang of regret hit my heart—he was back in his old-mage disguise. I wished he could walk by my side openly as the shifter Fenris, but since he'd been presumed dead in the Solantha quake, it was too much of a risk lest someone recognize him. He had already risked enough calling Solantha Palace as himself and was still going to need to sort that out.

Even so, I was tempted to take his hand and profess my love to him again... until I noticed Fenris's eyes were trained on the seagulls swirling about overhead.

"Best to keep things to mindspeak, for now," he warned, and I nodded.

We disembarked from the craft, our luggage in hand, and Fenris returned the keys to the yacht and settled with the rental company. We were just about to climb into one of the many steamcabs waiting outside the marina when an ether pigeon materialized directly in front of us.

"Oh!" I jumped back, pressing a hand against my pounding heart—I still wasn't used to seeing them. Fenris held out his arm as though he did this every day, and the pigeon perched on his forearm to deliver its message. It was from the Chief Mage—an order for us to come straight to the Mages Guild.

Fenris and I exchanged a look. "I wonder what happened that requires such urgency," I said as we climbed into the back of a steamcab. "Do you suppose something went wrong?"

"It's hard to say," Fenris said as the car slid into traffic. "Best not to worry or indulge in speculations and assumptions. We'll find out soon enough."

It was still early enough in the morning that the streets were snarled with traffic, and it took us nearly an hour to drive to Haralis Palace. We hurried up the steps as fast as we could without appearing unseemly after giving instructions to the driver to wait—he had our luggage in the trunk, and we could hardly bring it in with us. Hopefully he was honest.

I half expected the Chief Mage to make us wait, but to my pleasant surprise, his assistant ushered us into his private office almost immediately. Lord Zaran was seated behind a great oak desk with birds carved into the gleaming wood, a pair of spectacles perched on his nose as he reviewed a stack of documents on his desk. Standing next to him was a salt-and-pepper-haired mage in lime green robes who was jotting something down on a notepad—his secretary, I presumed.

"Thank you for coming so quickly," the Chief Mage said, setting aside whatever he was reading. "Have a seat."

We did so, and I forced my spine straight to keep from sinking into the chair cushion—it was softer than I'd anticipated. "Has your office finished the audit, then?" I asked, trying not to sound too eager.

"We have, but before I get into that, I must thank Mr. ar'Tarnis for opening my eyes to Miss Dorax's machinations." He turned his somber gaze toward Fenris. "I opened an investigation, and it has uncovered a series of irregularities that are most appalling. She has been placed under house arrest pending the completion of the investigation, upon which a panel of senior mages will come together to decide her fate."

"A wise decision," Fenris said, nodding. "I would post extra guards outside her doors. She seems like a devious woman, and I wouldn't put it past her to try to escape."

"Good thinking." The Chief Mage shook his head ruefully. "I cannot believe I allowed myself to be taken in by her—I should have known better, since she'd previously worked for that criminal who used to be the Chief Mage of Nebara. How is it that you, a stranger, were able to see through her when I could not?"

Fenris grimaced at the unwitting insult. "I have had the bad luck to tangle with her type on more than one occasion. When you live to be my age, you learn to spot the signs easily. I would not be surprised to learn that she has been angling for your position this entire time."

I bit back a smile, wondering how the Chief Mage would react if Fenris told him that he'd been that criminal mage and had found himself in the same position years ago. That it was his own experience that had given him such insight into Miss Dorax's character and had saved Lord Zaran from making the same mistakes.

"Yes, I suppose that makes sense, but..." The Chief Mage trailed off, cocking his head a little. "I can't help but feel as if we've met before, Mr. ar'Tarnis. Something about you seems familiar. Perhaps we've run across each other at a party, under a different guise?"

A chill ran down my spine, but Fenris merely laughed. "I assure you, Lord Zaran, if we had met before, I would have said so from the beginning," he said, lying with a perfectly straight face. "I am far too old for such games."

"Of course," the Chief Mage said, though he sounded mildly disappointed. He picked up a folder on his desk and turned to me. "Now, Miss Marton, on to the matter of your inheritance."

"Yes?" I sat up straighter—I'd begun to sink into the chair cushion again. "What have your people discovered?"

"Regretfully, our accountants found that a good third of your liquid assets, the bank accounts, and shares in various companies have been squandered by your faithless trustee and your greedy relatives." The Chief Mage sounded chagrined as he delivered the news. "They will be made to offer restitution, but their own assets are insufficient to cover the entire loss."

"Ah, so Mr. Ransome *was* dipping into my funds," I said as a wave of disappointment filled me. I'd been holding out hope that perhaps it was a misunderstanding, that he was better than this. But he had been the logical culprit—once again, Fenris was right.

"Yes, and he was also behind both attempts on your life," the Chief Mage said darkly. "He has been arrested, and after some days in a cell at the Enforcers Guild, is writing up a full confession as we speak. He truly believed that you were dead and therefore saw no harm in helping himself to some of your wealth." He scoffed. "When it turned out that you were still alive and well, Ransome panicked. In exchange for the confession, he will be sent to the mines for at least twenty years rather than face the death penalty. Either way, you will not see him again for the foreseeable future. All that remains is for you to decide whether you'd like for your relatives to be prosecuted, too."

I pursed my lips as I thought about it for a moment, then shook my head. "No, the loss of their income and social standing is punishment enough," I decided. Now that the truth was out, they would be disgraced. All the newspapers would have pounced on this story, eager to publish this latest society scandal, and nobody worth knowing would want to speak to them again. "There is no use wasting time and energy in prosecuting them—I'd like to get on with my life now."

"A mature decision," the Chief Mage said, smiling. "And it will save the taxpayers some money as well. But what exactly do you intend to do now that this is settled? Will you be moving back to Haralis?"

I sat back in my chair with a wide smile. "Not anytime soon, though I shall keep the Marton estate intact. As it turns out, there is a man in the town where I have been living whom I hope to marry," I said, winking at Fenris. His expression remained impassive, but I could have sworn I caught a twinkle in his eye. "My apprenticeship can wait for now."

After all, I would be able to learn from Fenris at my own pace and take the final tests with some other mage whenever we both felt I was ready.

The Chief Mage frowned. "Very well, though I must admit I am surprised. I would advise you not to put your training off too long—best to get it over with while you are young and the brain is still flexible. Are you sure you wouldn't like to stay here? There are several talented mages in Innarta who are very interested in teaching you now that they have learned of your ordeal. I could put you in touch with some of them."

I shrugged. "Perhaps I will take you up on that offer someday," I said, standing. "But my magic is under control, and I have waited this long—surely I can wait a few more years. For now, I intend to enjoy my life as Tamina Marton once more."

And with that, I bid the Chief Mage a good day and swept from Haralis Palace. I did not intend to come back for a good long time.

24

MINA

"I do wish you could stay a bit longer," Troina said, spooning up a bit of her cold cucumber soup. "Do you really have to leave so soon?"

I laughed. "It's been nearly four weeks since my hearing concluded," I said. We were sitting in the dining room of Troina's home, having a farewell lunch with Maxin, Baron, and a few other friends I'd become acquainted with in the past few weeks. While I enjoyed this last visit with my childhood friends, Fenris was picking up the tickets for our return trip. "I'm very glad I got to spend so much time with you all, but I really do need to get back to my life. I did have one before I came here, you know."

"Yes," Troina huffed, tossing a hank of her long hair over her shoulder. "But I will miss you, you know."

"We will *all* miss you," Maxin added, and the others voiced their agreement. "Your tenacity and courage has been an inspiration to us all, Mina. We could use more mages like you in our community."

I smiled softly. During the past few weeks, with Fenris's expert guidance, I had found caretakers for the various properties I now owned, drawn up a will, and taken care of other tedious issues that came with inheriting a vast fortune. I'd also spent lots of time with Troina and her friends, and I had grown to like them very much. Going out with mages my own age was a very nice change of pace. In between our fun-filled adventures, they'd even taught me some spells here and there to add to my growing repertoire.

But despite my growing fondness for them, I still missed Abbsville, and I had friends and clients waiting for me. I did not intend to move back there permanently, but I couldn't simply ignore the unfinished business I had there any more than Fenris could.

It was time to go home.

"I am surprised Secretary Dorax has been sent off to Dara for trial," Troina said, changing the subject. The news had made headlines in the paper that morning. "It was an open secret here that she was not above bribes, and she's not the first Finance Secretary who did so either. Nobody in the capital ever cared about it."

"The Chief Mage may be trying to recuse himself from the trial, since they worked so closely together," I speculated.

"No, it's this new Director of Federal Security," Maxin told us. "He is flexing his muscles, trying to establish his authority across the Federation. His agency claims to be in charge of all cases of corrupt mage officials."

"I'm not sure that is a good thing," Baron said, frowning. "We have state independence for a reason, after all, and who knows where it will end if the Federal government in Dara tries to dictate and meddle in our affairs?"

"You may be right," I said—Fenris held a very similar view on the subject. "But in this particular case, I am glad she is being sent far away. She did everything possible to ruin me."

"Have you seen your relatives since your hearing?" Maxin asked as he handed me a plate with salmon carpaccio to go with the bread I was buttering. "Vanley is missing from the social scene, so I don't know his feelings first-hand, but I imagine he isn't at all happy with you. Aren't you afraid he may plot revenge?"

"I have spent too many years being afraid of him," I declared. "When I finally came face-to-face with him at that party and he tried to accost me again, he turned out to be rather pathetic. I think I've outgrown him, and if he tries to hurt me again...well, I'm not without protection," I said with a smile. As a matter of fact, Fenris had been teaching me shielding and simple attack spells, so I would not be taken unawares should anyone else make an attempt on my life.

"You have certainly come into your own," Troina said, sounding proud of me. "I'm sure you will be fine. And anyway, your relatives have been ordered not to approach you, haven't they?"

"That's right," I confirmed. "I doubt they would want to see me anyway, not after being forced to pay restitution. They're practically copperless now."

"I don't doubt you could hold your own against Vanley now," Baron said. "My money is on you, but I expect he will just slink away to nurse his humiliation. He certainly won't be welcome in our circles again if I have anything to say to it."

"Yes, and he has no idea where I'm going, so there is no way for him to follow me," I said. At least not without hiring an investigator, which Vanley could not afford to do now that his family was broke.

"Speaking of which," Troina said, a little reproachfully, "*I* still have no idea where you are moving to either. Aren't you going to give me your address so we can keep in touch?"

"You can write to my old address here—all my mail will be forwarded," I told her. "I have not decided where I am settling yet, so there is no point in giving you my current address. I'll let you know as soon as I have found a place to settle permanently."

"It's a good idea, maintaining your privacy," Maxin said before Troina could protest. "You'd be overrun with begging letters and worse nuisances now that your case has been in the papers so prominently. But you'll still come and visit your properties here every now and again?"

"I will." Fenris was adamant that I periodically check in on my properties in person—at least once a year. *Without supervision, even the most trustworthy caretaker will eventually yield to temptation,* he'd said. "I'll call on you and Troina the next time I'm in town. I expect you will be married by then," I said with a smile.

"And have you finally got the keys to your mansion? What was the holdup there?" Troina asked.

"The Mages Guild insisted on a thorough inventory, and it took longer than expected since several items were missing. Small but precious things, like my late grandfather's golden mage staff. I doubt they will ever be recovered." The thought filled me with sadness—I would have treasured those heirlooms, which my grandmother had loved. But only a few things were missing. I'd received the keys to the place this morning, and Fenris and I were planning to drive out later in the afternoon.

"Well, your former trustee can reflect on his sins while he breaks stones in the mines," Troina said vindictively. "Though perhaps it was your aunt and uncle who took them. You can still change your mind and sue them, Mina."

"No, it's not worth the hassle. They've been punished enough." I took a sip from my glass of white wine, then changed the subject. "I'm glad we reconnected after all this time," I told them. "Haralis is no longer my home, but you have helped me recover many good memories of my time here—memories I'd forgotten about because of what Vanley and his family had done to me. Thanks to you all, I can now look back at Haralis with fondness instead of fear and anger."

"I wish we'd been able to help you when you were being harassed by Vanley, but I'm happy we were able to do something for you now," Troina said. "We'll miss you, but who knows, by the next century, you may change your mind and return here to your roots after all. Or your children may wish to settle in your ancestral home."

"Yes, that is why I am keeping the house," I admitted. "I do hope to have a family—several children, if possible."

Of course, first I had to persuade Fenris that children were a good idea. But judging by his actions lately, I had a feeling that wouldn't be very hard at all.

———

AFTER LUNCH, I took a steamcab back to the beachside hotel where we were still staying, then changed into a lavender linen gown that went well with my coloring. After some thought, I put on the matching amethyst jewelry I'd bought to go with it and took care arranging my hair. I felt like I needed to dress up a bit, almost as if I were going to visit my grandmother herself instead of the empty house that stood here in her wake.

"You look lovely," Fenris said as I met him out in the hall. He was in his old-mage guise again, so he did not touch or kiss me, but I could tell he wanted to from the look in his eye. "Are you ready?"

"Ready as I'll ever be," I said, taking his arm.

Fenris drove the rented steamcar as I gave directions. They were hardly needed, as he knew his way around Haralis pretty well by now. But the Marton family mansion, the same one he had pretended to want to buy not long ago, was outside the city right above the beach, and he was not as familiar with that area.

We parked outside and climbed out of the vehicle. I fumbled a little as I sought the right key to open the gate in the high metal fence, but at last it turned in the lock. For the first time in thirteen long years, I stood on my grandmother's property once more.

My place, now. I breathed in deeply and said nothing as Fenris looked around. Bees were humming, and a magpie eyed us curiously from the branch of an oak tree.

"Nobody is here today—we are quite alone," I said quietly. "The house is beyond those tall trees." I pointed to the path that led through the small grove.

"Let's go, then."

As we passed under the trees, Fenris dropped his mage disguise. I smiled, glad to have him beside me in his true form. We stopped once the two-story mansion was visible. It was exactly like I remembered it, covered in ivy, the sea behind it like a glittering frame. The house looked to be in decent shape, and the garden and lawns had been maintained, for which I was grateful. I didn't want to spend even more time here overseeing a restoration of the property.

"Ransome was quite right," Fenris said. "This house would not remain on the market for long. It would be a shame to sell it."

I smiled. "I agree. I have many fond memories of this place. I hope to share them with my children someday."

Fenris's eyes gleamed at the mention of children, but he said nothing, simply looping his arm through mine. Inside, we wandered through rooms that felt huge compared to anything

I'd inhabited over the last years and looked gloomy with the curtains drawn and the furniture shrouded in protective covers.

"This is a portrait of my grandmother," I said as we came to the dining room. She looked down from the canvas with her usual quizzical expression, a little larger than life.

Tears stung at the corners of my eyes, and my throat swelled as grief hit me unexpectedly. Fenris pulled me to his side with his strong right arm, and his warmth seeped into me, comforting me.

"She was lovely and clearly very intelligent," he said. "She would be proud of you, if she could see you now."

What would she have made of Fenris, though, I wondered? For mages of her generation, a relationship with a shifter would be shocking. But she and my parents were gone, and I had to use my own judgment, rely on my own feelings.

After showing him my former room and the huge kitchens, I opened the kitchen door into the back garden, which gently sloped downward to the beach. I was glad to see that the hired gardeners had taken diligent care of the rare trees, bushes, and flowers my ancestors had collected from all over the world.

"Let's go out again," I said, tugging Fenris by the hand. "I want to show you something in the garden."

Fenris followed me as I took the graveled path leading from the broad, shaded terrace to the left, winding between the profusion of flowers planted there. I took his hand as we reached a marble monument in the form of a portal looking down at the sea, with fluted columns on each side. White roses climbed up the columns. The gold-plated engraving on top was still as visible as the last time I had seen it.

"To the memory of Soran and Monissa Marton, lost at sea," I read aloud. Fenris silently put his arm around my shoulder, a steady rock as grief swelled within me again. "There never was a funeral, since their airship went down far from the shore," I whispered. "This is all I have to remember them by. I was so angry at them for leaving me to go off and die, but I guess that was childish. They would be here, if they could. To meet you, to make sure I was all right. It still seems unfair that their lives were cut so short." My voice broke, tears sliding down my cheeks.

"As long as you live, they will not be forgotten," Fenris said. He pulled me against his chest, holding me as I cried. Long minutes passed as I struggled with the grief. Eventually, I just let it go, let it all come out, until the well was finally empty and all that was left was the sound of Fenris's steady heartbeat beneath my cheek.

My rock. My anchor. My lover.

"I'm fine now." I sniffled as I finally pulled back. Fenris produced a handkerchief from his magical pocket, then led me over to sit on a marble bench that was set nearby in a rose bower, overlooking the shimmering waves. "It's just that being here brings it all back. The feeling of being alone, left behind, even while my grandmother lived. Sometimes I'd wished they had taken me with them on their ill-fated journey. I begged to go, you know, and they might have let me if I hadn't had some stupid exam in school that week." I wiped my eyes and handed the handkerchief back.

"That exam saved your life," Fenris said, cupping his face in my hands. His yellow eyes glowed with tenderness as he gazed at me. "I, for one, am very glad you did not join them."

He lowered his mouth to mine, and I sighed as I was swept into a deep, passionate kiss that made my toes curl. The grief was swept away as love and desire swelled in me, banishing the dark thoughts that had been clouding my mind. It was amazing how much better Fenris made me feel, simply by being here when I needed him.

After a few moments, we pulled back, sitting in companionable silence on the bench for a while, watching the glittering waves and the ships sailing past. "I'm so glad you're here with me," I said, leaning my head against his shoulder. "I don't know if I could have gotten through this without you. Ransome might have succeeded in killing me, or Miss Dorax would have branded me a swindler. Instead, both are in jail, and we are here. It seems like anything is possible when the one you love is beside you." I squeezed his arm affectionately.

Fenris smiled wryly. "It does, doesn't it? I have been telling myself that I had no right to tie you to me—a wanted man, over a century older, a shifter, a fugitive from justice. You know all the arguments why it would be dangerous, why you could do much better. But I love you, and I want to be with you forever."

He slid from the bench then, and my mouth dropped open as he knelt in front of me on the tidy gravel. "I know I am being selfish," he said as he pulled a small black box from his pocket, "but I cannot help myself. Will you marry me, Mina? Share my love, my home, despite everything?" His yellow eyes blazed with hope—and fear, I realized. Fear that I might reject him.

As if I ever could.

He popped open the box, and I gasped at the sight of the square-cut sapphire that sparkled in the afternoon sun like a tiny star. It was set in a band of white gold, and it was perfect.

"Of course I will," I said, beaming, and Fenris grinned. He slid the ring on my finger. It fit perfectly, and I sighed in admiration as I tilted my hand so it would sparkle in the light. "It's beautiful," I said, and then threw myself into his arms for another kiss. He growled as he pulled me to the ground, and I rolled onto my back, urging him atop me.

"I want a life with you, Fenris," I panted against his mouth as he bunched the flowing skirts of my dress around my legs. "A family, with at least three children."

"Nothing would make me happier," he assured me, a wicked glint in his eye. "What do you say we start right now?"

He kissed me again, and I abandoned myself to the moment, in wholehearted agreement.

———

A GOOD WHILE LATER, Fenris and I finally collected ourselves. We left the grounds with the sun setting behind us. I was giddy with happiness as we headed for where we'd parked the steamcar, the ring a welcome weight on my finger and my heart light with joy. Fenris had the presence of mind to change back into his mage disguise before we walked out, but for once, I didn't care. I knew the man inside loved me, and he was still in there regardless of who he looked like on the outside.

But as we approached the steamcar, the joy in my heart died a little. Vanley was leaning against the hood of the car, scowling as we approached. Fenris stiffened at my side, but he schooled his features into casual indifference, so I did the same.

"Don't let him bully you," Fenris warned in mindspeak.

"So you think you won," Vanley sneered as we stopped in front of him.

I raised an eyebrow. "There is no question about it, cousin," I said, flicking a loose strand of hair over my shoulder. "But then again, there was never any kind of contest between us, as far as I'm concerned. You mean nothing to me."

"It's *your* fault my parents have cut off my allowance," Vanley hissed. "And worse, they're blaming *me* for it."

"You're finally suffering the consequences of your actions?" I said in mock surprise. "That is excellent news."

"I could annihilate you with a single Word," Vanley said, rising to his full height. I lifted my chin to meet his gaze, refusing to be cowed by his threatening tone. As I stared him down, I saw a flicker of unease in his eyes as he briefly glanced toward Fenris. I smiled—he was not nearly as confident as he sounded.

"Try it," I challenged. "I've been looking for an excuse to finally get you back after all these years."

"Get *me* back?" Vanley sputtered, his face turning purple. "After what you did?"

Fenris stepped forward, subtly putting his big body between Vanley and me. "I would be very careful about what you say next," he said quietly, his voice ominous. "The lady is under my protection. Not that she needs much protection from a coward who only attacks young girls who cannot fight back," he added, "but I thought I should warn you all the same."

"I didn't attack anyone," Vanley protested. "I was behaving like any boy would! My 'harassment,' as Mina calls it, was no more than a bit of innocent ragging. You were so pale and pathetic you practically asked for it," he spat at me.

I opened my mouth to respond, but Vanley made a vicious slashing motion with his hand, and a wave of fire hurtled toward me. Fear leapt into my throat, but even so, I kept enough of my wits about me to conjure the shielding spell that Fenris had taught me. The fire bounced harmlessly off it, and Fenris extinguished it before it could spread elsewhere.

"Enough," Fenris growled, his eyes blazing with anger. He made a quick gesture with his hands and spoke an incantation, the Words too fast for me to catch. Magic exploded out of his hand and hit Vanley square in the chest. Vanley opened his mouth, a cry on his lips, but his features froze in a comical expression of horror, as did the rest of his body.

He'd become a living statue.

"Your punishment is long overdue," Fenris said with icy disdain. I thought he was just going to leave Vanley like that, which was good enough for me, but he murmured another spell instead before he released my cousin.

"What—" I began, wondering if Fenris had decided to let him off. But Vanley slowly reached up, and to my amazement, tore out a chunk of his thick, chestnut-brown hair. He yelped as the clump of hair came free, and then he did it again, and then again. Tears streamed down his cheeks the entire time, and blood began to run down from his scalp and into his eyes, but he did not stop.

"Come now," Fenris said, taking me by the arm and leading me to the car. "Let Vanley administer the rest of his punishment in peace."

"What did you do to him?" I asked curiously as I looked at Vanley over my shoulder. I had never heard of a spell that caused someone to tear their own hair out, but then again, I was a novice. Vanley was sobbing openly now, his shoulders shaking, yet I felt no pity as I watched him suffer. After all, he had felt none for me. "And how long is it going to affect him?"

Fenris shrugged. "Right now, until he is bald—but it's going to recur whenever he bullies anyone else, for seven years. It is an old Manucan curse I found in an ancient manuscript."

"It seems a little cruel," I remarked as we got into the car, but I wasn't about to tell him to stop it. It wasn't going to kill Vanley, after all, and if a curse was what it took to save others from being preyed on, it seemed a small price to pay.

"After everything he did to you, your cousin is lucky he got away with his life," Fenris said darkly as we drove away.

I reached for his hand. "Thank you for defending me," I said softly.

He smiled. "You hardly needed it. That was a very good shielding spell you did."

"Thanks," I said, beaming. "I think I'm ready for you to teach me that freezing spell you just did on Vanley. Does it work on animals, too? It would be invaluable when dealing with rabid skunks or enraged bulls."

We spent the rest of the car ride talking about magical theory and our upcoming departure. And as we crossed over the bridge to Haralis, looking out over the glittering waves, the joy and satisfaction I'd felt when leaving the mansion returned tenfold. So long as I had Fenris, there truly was nothing to fear anymore. I had his back, and he would always have mine.

A few days later, I found myself standing outside Barrla's door, ready to pick up the young tomcat I'd left with her for safekeeping. For the time being, I was glad to be back in the quaint small town I'd started to consider home, though Fenris and I were planning to relocate within the next year or so once we decided where we wanted to bring up our future family.

"Mina!" The door flew open, and Barrla enveloped me in a hug. "You're back! Finally!"

"Got in last night," I managed as she squeezed the air out of my lungs. Despite the discomfort, I wrapped my arms around her and returned the squeeze—I hadn't realized until we'd begun the journey home that I'd missed her. "How is the cat?"

"He's taken over the place," Barrla said as she herded me into the house. It was a spacious three-bedroom, brightly decorated with large, open windows that let in lots of light. Not the biggest house in Abbsville, but certainly one of the nicer ones—as the owner of the general store, Barrla's father could afford it. "I'm not sure you're getting him back."

Sure enough, the tom was sunning himself on a fat pillow on the blue-gray couch, and he swatted at my hand when I reached for him. "He's gotten so big," I said as I sat down on the cushion next to him. "Almost full-grown, now."

"Yes. And he's become very attached to my mother," Barrla said fondly, scratching him behind the ears. "She's named him Oscar."

"Well, if she's named him, then I suppose she ought to keep him," I said ruefully. "It's for the best," I added when Barrla looked as though she were about to apologize. "He never liked Fenris much, and if I have to choose between the two, Fenris wins hands down."

"Can't say I blame you," Barrla said with a grin. She sat down in the chair across from me and crossed her legs, causing the pale pink skirts of her dress to ripple. "I wonder when Marris is coming back," she said, the expression on her face turning wistful. "I do hope he's safe."

"I'm sure he's fine," I said—Fenris had filled me in on what was going on with Marris on our journey to Haralis. "He's a resourceful young man."

"He is, isn't he?" Barrla said admiringly. "I've had a lot of time to think about everything Fenris told me—how Marris risked his neck to give gold to our poor neighbors in the dead of night and is now on the run because of it. It reminds me of one of my favorite books, *The Secret Knight*."

"Ah, yes, I remember that one." Barrla had been obsessed with it—another one of her shifter novels, of course, about a fugitive with a golden heart.

"Marris might not be a shifter," Barrla went on, "but he is certainly heroic, and since you've taken the only shifter in town, he's the next best thing. He'd better come back soon, though," she added with a huff, crossing her arms. "He owes me a date."

"He's crazy about you, Barrla," I said gently, sensing the undercurrent of nerves in my friend's flippant tone. I knew that beneath her posturing, she was deeply worried that Marris might not come back to her. "I'm sure he's just as eager to get back to you as you are to see him."

"Yes, I know you're right," Barrla said, sighing a little. But then she seemed to gather herself. "Enough about my worries, though. Let's get back to you and Fenris. Are you two truly a couple now?"

"Yes." I beamed, my heart filling with joy as I remembered the moment Fenris had finally told me that he loved me. "We're engaged."

"By the Ur-God!" Barrla shrieked, clapping her hands and scaring Oscar. He shot off the couch and into the kitchen. "Is that what the new ring on your finger is about, then?" She glanced down at my left hand, where the sapphire now sparkled.

"Yes." I grinned foolishly as I held it up. The other ring that had the illusion spell tied to it was on my right hand—I was still attached to it, for sentimental reasons. After all, both were from my beloved. "It's beautiful, isn't it?"

"Absolutely gorgeous," Barrla declared, and if there was the barest hint of envy in her voice, we both chose to ignore it.

After I finished my visit with Barrla, I returned to my own house to finish packing up my things, then loaded them up into my small rig and headed for Fenris's farm. Now that I'd told Barrla, word of our engagement would spread like wildfire, so I saw no harm in living with him even though it wasn't quite proper. I was very much looking forward to waking up in bed with Fenris every morning. Soon, we would be moving to a bigger, more luxurious house that we could fill with children and pets.

When I came into the farmhouse, I was greeted by the sound of a hammer. Dumping my belongings in the bedroom, I followed the hammering to a room in the back, which Fenris and I were converting into a temporary surgery. He was shirtless as he worked, installing a couple of large sinks and cabinets to hold my instruments and medications. The metal table for exams and surgeries, along with the cages, would have to be transported later.

I leaned against the doorjamb for a moment, watching his back muscles flex as he pounded in yet another nail.

"How did your visit with Barrla go?" he asked without turning around, and I smiled. Of course he'd sensed me—he probably had known I was here before I'd even walked into the house.

"Well enough. The cat is staying there."

"Thank the Lady for that," he said fervently, putting down the hammer so he could kiss me. I settled my hands on his broad shoulders and felt dampness—he must have been working quite hard if he was starting to sweat.

"As much as I enjoy seeing you like this," I said, pulling back, "wouldn't it be faster for you to use magic?"

Fenris shrugged. "I like working with my hands from time to time," he said. "Although now that I think about it, it uses more energy than magic does. I'm starved."

He took a break, and I made sandwiches and poured cold milk for the two of us. As we sat at the kitchen table, enjoying our simple meal, we discussed our plans.

"How long do you think we'll stay here in Abbsville?" I asked. "You only just moved here, but I can't imagine raising a family together here, especially since our children will undoubtedly all be mages."

"Oh, we definitely won't be raising children here," Fenris agreed. "This place is far too humble for a lady of your means. Besides, the Watawis mages are not very progressive and will become suspicious if you marry a shifter."

"True enough," I said. "But where will we move? I suppose

Solantha would be a good choice, but since you can't return there..."

"We'll figure it out when the time comes," Fenris assured me. "For now, we ought to focus on the wedding. We'll need to find a mage temple, and someone willing to—"

We were interrupted by a knock on the door, and Fenris's eyes flew wide with pleased surprise. "It's Marris!" he exclaimed, jumping out of his chair. I rushed to the door with him to answer it.

"Courier service," Marris said with a grin as we opened the door. He was dressed in a dusty white shirt and khakis, a large wooden box sitting at his feet.

"Marris!" I flung my arms around him in a quick hug, relieved—we'd known each other quite a while now, and I was very happy he'd returned safe. "Barrla's been pining for you, you know," I said with a wink as I pulled back.

Marris's grin turned downright devious. "I suppose I'll have to go and reassure her that I'm all right," he said as Fenris pounced on the box like a man in the desert who had just stumbled upon a jug of fresh water. "You need any help with that?"

"Not at all," Fenris said, carrying it inside with ease. "Why don't you come inside and have something to eat? You look parched."

I fixed Marris up with a sandwich and milk while Fenris set the box on the living room floor and tore it open with the claw side of the hammer. "Ahh..." he said with a smile as he began to lovingly unpack the contents—a series of leather-bound texts, some of which looked quite old. "I cannot tell you how much I've missed these."

"You planning on putting those up here in the living room?" Marris asked. "Because they might attract the wrong kind of attention if you get visitors."

"He has a safe place planned for them," I said wryly. During the flight to Haralis, Fenris had been sketching out plans for a hidden bookshelf that would stand behind a sliding wall, and he was eager to start the project now that we were home. In fact, I wouldn't be surprised if he abandoned my surgery entirely to start on it, now that the books were here. In the meantime, they would sit in a chest hidden beneath the floorboards, where he'd already placed the ones he'd bought during our trip. All these were only temporary measures, since we were not planning to live here for much longer. I decided that whatever house we bought together should have a big library for normal books, as well as a hidden bookroom for Fenris's magic collection.

"Did you have much trouble retrieving these?" Fenris asked as he carefully continued to unpack the trunk, smiling at favorites. He was clearly eager to delve into their pages, and I couldn't help grinning—he was like a child in a toy store.

Marris shook his head. "I found out that somebody had been watching the box a few months back, but only for a week or so, and then they left. There was definitely nobody snooping around when I arrived."

I bit my lip at that—Marris was naïve when it came to the ways of mages. It was possible someone could have been watching from afar or even placed a tracker on the box.

"I've checked already—the box has not been magically tampered with," Fenris told me via mindspeak as our eyes met.

I nodded subtly, then forced myself to put it out of my mind. There was little point in worrying about it right now, and I didn't want to taint this otherwise happy moment. "Did you have any adventures along the way?" I asked.

"Not exactly, but I visited some old Resistance buddies here and there," he said. "A few of them were getting ready to travel to Solantha at the end of the summer—there's supposed to be a big society wedding, and all the most important mages in the Federation are going. It's a prime opportunity for a strike. They looked forward to reversing our setbacks and winning a decisive victory when the mages least expect it."

Fenris dropped the book he was holding, and it landed on the floor with an ominous thud. "Did you find out who was organizing the operation?" he asked sharply.

"No, and I don't know who the target is supposed to be either," Marris said. "I had half a mind to join in if it turned out to be too dangerous for me to come back—it sounds like fun, everyone getting together one last time. If the mages are trying to catch me anyway for minting those gold coins, I might as well get my revenge in first," he added, a little viciously. "We might get to strike at the Minister himself!"

"Don't be foolish," Fenris said sternly, all traces of delight gone from his expression. "Disrupting a wedding is very bad luck. Besides, haven't we agreed that our goal should be preventing injustice rather than lashing out at mages in general? You wouldn't get at the Minister without killing lots of innocent bystanders."

"Your goal?" I echoed, looking back and forth between them as Marris winced guiltily. "What in Recca are you two talking about?"

"Er, you mean you haven't told her about the League of Justice?" Marris asked Fenris.

"I've been preoccupied," Fenris said dryly.

I stared. "The League of Justice?"

Fenris sighed, then proceeded to explain to me about the new group Marris, Cobil, and Roth had formed, and how they'd asked Fenris to join right before our trip to Haralis.

"Well, if there is going to be such a league, then I demand to be enrolled at once," I said, torn between amusement and genuine interest. I wasn't sure what Marris thought he could accomplish, but with Fenris's level head to keep them on course, perhaps they could actually do some good. We certainly could not let Marris go off to join some doomed and, from the sound of it, extremely dangerous terrorist attack in Solantha. "I have a feeling Barrla will want to be a part of it, too, once she ferrets this out of you."

Marris chuckled. "I don't want to get her involved with anything dangerous, but knowing her, she'll find a way to force herself in anyway."

Eventually, Marris took his leave, eager to finally go and see his lady love. As soon as he was gone, Fenris turned to me, a grave expression on his handsome face.

"I am very concerned about this possible plot," he said. "If there is any threat to Iannis and Sunaya's wedding, I must warn them immediately. I'll need to go to the inn and use the phone booth."

"You mean you're just going to call them?" I asked incredulously. "What about going to help them?"

Fenris froze. I could tell he wanted to do exactly that, but was torn. "If I were to go," he said after a moment, "I should go alone —I cannot put you in harm's way, in case I am recognized. If I am arrested, you might be caught up in the backlash."

"Don't be ridiculous," I said, crossing my arms over my chest. "*Of course* I'm going with you. I would very much like to meet your friends. After all you have been through together, Lord Iannis isn't going to have you arrested if you return. You'll just go in disguise, anyway, like in Haralis."

"It is doable," Fenris murmured, a faraway look in his eyes that told me he was already plotting it. "But it could be very dangerous." His gaze sharpened. "The Resistance can be cutthroat in its methods—you have not truly experienced what they are capable of. And mages are just as dangerous when cornered."

"If that's the case, it's even more important that I be by your side," I insisted, slipping a hand in his. "I'm not about to let the man I love go charging off into trouble while I sit at home and twiddle my thumbs. The only way you would convince me to do that is if we had a houseful of babies and wolf cubs."

Fenris's expression softened, and I was rewarded with a reluctant smile. "I suppose I ought to marry you soon, then, so we can get started on that," he said, leaning in for a kiss.

"Mmm," I said in agreement as I kissed him back, sliding my arms around him. Fenris might try to argue again later, but I knew he wouldn't be able to resist for long. I was very much looking forward to visiting Solantha despite the possible danger —I'd heard it was a fascinating city, and besides, it had a mage temple. Who was to say that Iannis and Sunaya were the only ones getting married there soon?

To be continued...

Fenris and Mia's story will conclude in SAVED BY MAGIC, Book 3 in The Baine Chronicles: Fenris's story!

If you'd like to be notified when the next book comes out, make sure you're subscribed to Jasmine's newsletter!

CLICK HERE TO SIGN UP

GLOSSARY

Abbsville: a small town in the state of Watawis, population ca. 800 including the surrounding farms.

Abbsville Book Club: popular with the local ladies. Among its members are Mina Hollin, Barrla Kelling, Mrs. Cattin, Mrs. Vamas, Mrs. Tamil, Mrs. Bartow, Mrs. Staffer, Mrs. Canterbew and ancient Mrs. Harpton.

Ackleberry Farm: a farm outside Abbsville that Fenris has bought from the Ackleberry family, sight unseen, under the name of J.F. Shelton.

Apprenticeship: all mages are expected to complete an apprenticeship with some master mage, that usually lasts from age fifteen to about twenty-five. Only after the final exam may they use colorful robes, and are considered legally of age. Otherwise they only attain their majority at age thirty.

ar': suffix in some mages' family names, that denotes they are of noble birth, and can trace their descent to one of Resinah's twelve disciples.

Baine, Sunaya: a half-panther shifter, half-mage who used to hate mages and has a passion for justice. Because magic is forbidden to all but the mage families, Sunaya was forced to keep her abilities a secret until she accidentally used them to defend herself in front of witnesses. Rather than condemn her to death, the Chief Mage, Iannis ar'Sannin, chose to take her on as his apprentice, and eventually his fiancée. She struggles to balance her shifter and mage heritage.

Baine, Rylan: Sunaya Baine's cousin, and like her, a panther shifter. An active member of the Resistance, with the rank of Captain, he was captured and imprisoned during the uprising in Solantha, but ultimately pardoned.

Baron: a young mage, friend of Troina and Maxin, that Mina meets in Haralis.

Barnas: a town in the state of Uton, home to a large wolf shifter clan.

Barrla, see under Kelling, Barrla.

Benefactor: the anonymous, principal source of financial support to the Resistance, who was eventually unmasked as the socialite Thorgana Mills (now deceased).

Black Horse: the best hotel in Haralis.

Boccol: family name of a wealthy farmer family in Abbsville.

Branis, Garton: false name that Fenris uses to inquire about Mina's family mansion.

Brialtha: a young mage Mina meets at a party in Haralis.

Canalo: one of the fifty states making up the Northia Federation, located on the West Coast of the Northia Continent.

Cantorin, Allira: Mina's aunt and closest surviving relative, sister of her deceased mother.

Cantorin, Bobb: Mina's uncle by marriage.

Cantorin, Vanley: Mina's cousin, the reason she ran away from her guardians' home at fifteen.

Cattin, Mrs: wife of Abbsville's pastor (for the Ur-god temple), a leading member of the local book club.

Central Continent: the largest of the continents on Recca, spanning from Garai in the east to Castalis in the west.

Chief Mage: head of one of the fifty states of the Northia Federation, usually addressed as "Lord Firstname". The Chief Mages come together as the Convention every other year, usually in the capital Dara.

Cobil: childhood friend and co-conspirator of Marris Dolan and Rotharius.

ar'Contir, Haltinas: a mage employed by the Legal Secretary of the Watawis Mages' Guild.

Convention: the assembly of all Chief Mages and highest authority in the Federation.

Creator: the ultimate deity, worshipped by all three races under different names.

Croialis: a poison made from the seed of a tropical plant, popular for assassinations as it is not susceptible to magical healing.

Dara: capital of the Northia Federation, located on the east coast of the Northia Continent.

Darina: a young mage Mina meets at a party in Haralis.

Dira: Lord Iannis's principal secretary in the Mages Guild offices in Solantha.

Dolan, Marris: a young Abbsville farmer who has spent some time fighting for the Resistance.

Dolan, Dana, Roglar, and **Decrin:** the younger siblings of Marris Dolan, living with their widowed mother at the Dolan Farm.

Dorax, Gelisia: an ambitious mage official, formerly Finance Secretary in Nebara, and later in Innarta.

Faricia: a large continent that straddles the North and South hemispheres, located south of the Central Continent's western region. Inhabited by many different nations and tribes; partly inaccessible to foreign travelers.

Fenris aka "Jalen Fenris Shelton": a clanless wolf shifter of unusual antecedents, close friend and confidant of Chief Mage

Iannis ar'Sannin and Sunaya Baine, but currently striking out on his own.

Finance Secretary: in each state, the Chief Mages are assisted by Secretaries (Finance, Legal, Agriculture, etc.) some of whom may eventually achieve the rank of Chief Mage themselves.

Foggart, Davin: Constable in Abbsville, the only local law enforcement officer.

Handmar, Mr. and Mrs., Hartley and **Kelton:** a breeder of horses in Watawis, his wife and twin sons.

Haralis: a port city on the east coast and capital of Innarta, one of the most prosperous states in the Northia Federation.

Haralis Monitor: main local newspaper of Haralis, the capital of Innarta.

Harmon, Tuala: name of an elderly acquaintance Mina's late grandmother, that she uses when she pretends to be a fully trained mage herself.

Hollin, Mina, aka **Tamina Marton,** aka **Tuala Harmon:** Mina's original name is Tamina Marton, and from childhood she was called "Mina" by her friends and family. After running away as a teenager, she used the name Mina Hollin.

Iannis: see ar'Sannin, Iannis.

Innarta: one of the fifty states of the Northia Federation, where Mina's family hails from.

Julon: owner of Abbsville's only inn.

Karadin, Janis: Legal Secretary of the Watawis government.

Kelling, Barrla: Mina's best friend in Abbsville, who works in her parents' general store and loves shifter romances.

Kelling, Mr. and Mrs. Sallia: Barrla and Terad's parents, owners of Abbsville's general store.

Kelling, Terad: Barrla's younger brother.

Lady, the: mages refer to the First Mage, Resinah, as the Lady, most often in the phrase "by the Lady!"

Loranian: the difficult, secret language of magic that all mages are required to master.

ar'Lutis, Fennias: pseudonym Fenris used among the Watawis mages.

Mages Guild: the governmental organization that rules the mages in each state, and supervises the other races. The headquarters are usually in the same building as the Palace of the local Chief Mage, to whom the Guild is subordinate.

Magorah: the god of the shifters, associated with the moon.

Makar: a gelding Fenris buys from Handmar, the local horse breeder.

Mallas, Zaran: Chief Mage of the state of Innarta, resides in the capital Haralis.

Manucan: the language of Manuc, an island country northwest of the Central Continent.

Marton, Soran and **Monissa:** Mina's late parents, who died in an airship accident.

Marton, Tamina: Mina's original name.

Maxin: a young mage and childhood friend of Mina's, engaged to her friend Troina.

ar'Mees, Clostina: a young mage working for the Watawis Mages' Guild, granddaughter of the Chief Mage.

ar`Mees, Lord Zander and Lady Marilla: the Chief Mage of Watawis and his wife.

Midnight: a stallion that Fenris buys soon after arriving in Watawis.

Mills, Thorgana: socialite and former owner of a news media conglomerate as well as numerous other companies. After being exposed as the Benefactor she was imprisoned. She managed to escape, but died around the time of the Solantha earthquake.

Mina, see under Hollin, Mina.

Minister, the: the mage who presides the Convention of

Chief Mages, and coordinates the affairs of the Northia Federation between sessions, particularly foreign relations. The office is currently held by Zavian Graning.

Murmuzel: local name for a type of squirrel prevalent near Haralis.

Nebara: one of the fifty states making up the Northia Federation, located north of Canalo, and Fenris's home state.

Northia Federation: a federation consisting of fifty states that cover almost the entire northern half and middle of the Western Continent.

Northian: the main language spoken in the Northia Federation.

Orkon: see under Trulian, Orkon.

Oscar: the name Mrs. Kelling gives to the tomcat Mina entrusted to Barrla.

Osero: one of the fifty states of the Northia Federation, located north of Canalo on the continent's west coast.

Pandanum: a base metal used, inter alia, for less valuable coins.

Polar: see under ar'Tollis, Polar.

Provence: family name of a goat breeder, one of Mina's clients.

Ransome, Domich: a mage, and lawyer and trustee to the Marton family, in Haralis; in charge of Mina's inheritance since her grandmother's death.

Recca: the world of humans, mages and shifters.

Resinah: the first mage, whose teachings are of paramount spiritual importance for the mages. Her statue can be found in the mage temples, which are off-limits to non-mages and magically hidden from outsiders.

Resistance: a movement of revolutionaries planning to overthrow the mages and take control of the Northia Federation, financially backed by the Benefactor. Over time they became bolder and more aggressive, using terrorist attacks with civilian casualties, as well as assassination. The discovery that the Benefactor and the human leaders of the Resistance were planning to turn on the shifters once the mages were defeated dealt a blow to the unity of the movement, but its human component is far from completely defeated.

Rice, Hulam: a journalist working for the Haralis Monitor.

Roor, Ilain: a young farmer in Abbsville, son of Mrs. Roor.

Rotharius aka Roth: together with Cobil, friend and companion of Marris Dolan.

Rylan: see under Baine, Rylan.

ar'Sannin, Iannis: Chief Mage of Canalo. He resides in the capital city of Solantha, from which he runs Canalo as well as the Mages Guild with the help of his deputy and Secretaries. Originally a native of Manuc, a country located across the Eastern Sea.

Sarman: false name Fenris used to store some of his most precious old books in Osero.

Shelton: the false family name under which Fenris has bought Ackleberry farm in Abbsville.

Shifter: a human who can change into animal form and back by magic; they originally resulted from illegal experiments by mages on ordinary humans.

Silver: the metal is toxic to shifters, and burns their skin when they touch it. It is nevertheless used for coins in the Federation.

Smorth, Ria: former fiancée of Cobil's brother.

Solantha: the capital of Canalo State, a port city on the west coast of the Northia continent. Seat of Chief Mage Iannis ar'Sannin and the Canalo Mages Guild, and home of Sunaya Baine.

Sunaya: see under Baine, Sunaya.

ar'Tarnis, Yoron: Fenris's pseudonym in Haralis, to go with his disguise as an old mage from the Central Continent.

Testing: human and shifter schoolchildren in the Northia Federation are tested for magic at least twice during their schoolyears, and a positive result will normally lead to the magic wipe (often with permanent mental damage.)

Thorgana: see under Mills, Thorgana.

Tilin, Mr.: the Abbsville carpenter.

Tira: the beloved, thirteen-year old mastiff of the Dolan family.

ar'Tollis, Polar: former Chief Mage of Nebara, who vanished after being condemned to death by the Convention.

Toring, Garrett: mage, Federal Director of Security, former Federal Secretary of Justice; an ambitious high official in the Federal government.

Troina: a young mage, and childhood friend of Mina's from her schooldays.

ar'Trud, Maggals: a deceased Osero mage who Mina pretends used to be her master, when she claims to be Tuala Harmon.

Trulian, Orkon and **Tridaris:** Orkon Trulian led the first settlers to what is now the state of Innarta. Mina is descended from him through his daughter Tridaris.

Ur-God: the name the humans call the Creator by.

Uton: one of the fifty states of the Northia Federation.

Vanley: see under Cantorin, Vanley.

Watawis: one of the fifty states of the Northia Federation, landlocked, in the mountainous northwest. It is one of the least populated and poorest of the fifty states.

Willowdale: capital of the state of Watawis, seat of its Chief Mage and government.

Words: Loranian formulas used by mages for almost all standard spells.

Yoron: see under ar'Tarnis, Yoron.

ABOUT THE AUTHOR

JASMINE WALT is obsessed with books, chocolate, and sharp objects. Somehow, those three things melded together in her head and transformed into a desire to write, usually fantastical stuff with a healthy dose of action and romance. Her characters are a little (okay, a lot) on the snarky side, and they swear, but they mean well. Even the villains sometimes.

When Jasmine isn't chained to her keyboard, you can find her practicing her triangle choke on the jujitsu mat, spending time with her family, or binge-watching superhero shows on Netflix.

Want to connect with Jasmine? You can find her on Instagram at @jasmine.walt, on Facebook, or at www.jasminewalt.com.

ALSO BY JASMINE WALT

The Baine Chronicles: Fenris's Story:

Forsaken by Magic (Novella)

Fugitive by Magic

Claimed by Magic

Saved by Magic (Coming Soon!)

The Baine Chronicles Series:

Burned by Magic

Bound by Magic

Hunted by Magic

Marked by Magic

Betrayed by Magic

Deceived by Magic

Scorched by Magic

Taken by Magic (Coming Soon!)

The Nia Rivers Adventures:

Coauthored with Ines Johnson

Dragon Bones

Demeter's Tablet

Templar Scrolls—Coming Soon!

The Gatekeeper Chronicles:

Coauthored with Debbie Cassidy

Marked by Sin

Hunted by Sin

Claimed by Sin

66145889R00119

Made in the USA
Columbia, SC
16 July 2019